The Cowboy's Road Home

Cowboys of Whistle Rock Ranch, Book One
Contemporary Western Romance

SHIRLEEN DAVIES

Book Series by Shirleen Davies

Historical Western Romances

Redemption Mountain
MacLarens of Fire Mountain Historical
MacLarens of Boundary Mountain

Romantic Suspense

Eternal Brethren Military Romantic Suspense
Peregrine Bay Romantic Suspense

Contemporary Western Romance

Cowboys of Whistle Rock Ranch
MacLarens of Fire Mountain Contemporary
Macklins of Whiskey Bend

The best way to stay in touch is to subscribe to my newsletter. Go to my Website ***www.shirleendavies.com*** and fill in your email and name in the Join My Newsletter boxes.

That's it!

Avalanche Ranch Press, LLC
PO Box 12618
Prescott, AZ 86304

The Cowboy's Road Home is a work of fiction. Names, characters, places, and incidents are either products of the author's imagination or used fictitiously. Any resemblance to actual events, locales, or persons, living or dead, is wholly coincidental.

Book design and conversions by Joseph Murray at 3rdplanetpublishing.com

Cover design by Sweet 'n Spicy Designs

ISBN: 978-1-947680-70-8

I care about quality, so if you find something in error,
please contact me via email at
shirleen@shirleendavies.com

Description

**Second chances aren't a sure thing.
Not when sparks fly between the perfect woman
and a devoted cowboy whose father
is determined to keep them apart.**

It's been eight years since Wyatt Bonner left Whistle Rock Ranch.

After two college degrees and loads of experience helping to run his uncle's dude ranch, he's back and ready to take his place beside his father. Sunrise to sunset, he's all business, hardworking, and dedicated to the family's horse breeding operation—until Daisy Raines bursts back into his life.

A successful businesswoman, Daisy's never forgotten her first love. Learning Wyatt has returned to Brilliance, Wyoming, and the family ranch, she faces a hard truth. She still loves the handsome, sometimes cocky cowboy.

After eight years, she expects little, and is surprised when Wyatt makes it clear he wants another chance. The independent Daisy is all in until a significant obstacle blocks their growing relationship.

There's no sure path to a second chance. Not when Wyatt's father is dead set against a union including Daisy.

The Cowboy's Road Home, book one in the Cowboy's of Whistle Rock Ranch Contemporary Western Romance series, is a clean and wholesome, full-length novel with an HEA and no cliffhanger.

The Cowboy's Road Home

Chapter One

Bozeman, Montana
Early October...

Wyatt Bonner swiped a gloved hand over his face, angry at himself, and the forecast he'd read before dawn. The wind whipped around the small group of riders, slamming snow against their clothes and unprotected faces.

The baseball caps, jeans, and lightweight jackets meant for a brisk fall day were inadequate against the freak, early winter storm. He'd guided the two women and three men on a six mile ride. It was the last ride of the season at his uncle's dude ranch before Wyatt packed his belongings and returned to Whistle Rock Ranch after an eight year absence.

"What a way to finish up in Montana," he muttered to himself, clamping down his hat when a gust almost swept it away. "We're almost there. Keep your head down and let the horse take you home." His voice rose to a shout as another gust hit them.

Feeling his phone vibrate, he drew it from a pocket, almost dropping it. His uncle. He should've expected the call, but he'd been too busy calming down the guests and keeping them moving after the storm hit. Wyatt accepted the call.

"We're about fifteen minutes out, Uncle Emmett."

"Your aunt has coffee, hot chocolate, spice cake, and a roaring fire ready in the main lodge. How bad is it?"

"Not good. Weather service sure didn't show a storm building."

"You got that right, son. We'll be waiting for you."

Wyatt rode to the back of the group before returning to his spot at point, shouting encouragement to each rider as he passed. Of the five, just one concerned him. The woman had arrived at the ranch a day late, insisted on changing her assigned cabin, and complained about the food at every meal. No one understood why she'd signed up for a week at their Gallatin Dude Ranch.

The same as the others, she'd be gone tomorrow afternoon. Uncle Emmett had every expectation she'd leave a scathing review. So be it. They couldn't please everyone.

At the sight of the ranch house up ahead, Wyatt tore his hat from his head, waving it in the air.

"Yeehaw!"

All five riders lifted their heads at his yell, four mimicking him, with broad smiles on their faces. The fifth shook her head, staring back down at the saddlehorn.

Three wranglers awaited them. Less than ten minutes after arriving, the riders were in the main lodge, sipping hot chocolate within feet of the fireplace.

"You ready to head home tomorrow, Wyatt?" Uncle Emmett stood next to him, resignation and sadness clear in the lines around his mouth and eyes.

"The truck is packed. All I have to do is load Mighty Quinn."

Emmett sipped the strong coffee he preferred. "What time you taking off?"

Wyatt turned to face his uncle. Older than his father by a few years, Emmett was what people expected to see when imagining a cowboy. Tanned, leathery skin spoke of years of hard work around the ranch. It was Emmett's eyes which drew people to him. Dignity, wisdom, and innate honesty radiated from deep caramel brown pools, earning the trust of those who knew him.

"Before sunup."

"We're gonna miss you, son. Your Aunt Lucinda will have a real hard time. Make sure you spend some time with her tonight."

"Yes, sir. I'd never leave without saying goodbye. I probably haven't said it enough, but I appreciate all you and Aunt Lucinda have done for me the past eight years. When Pop said I'd be coming here after graduating high school, I didn't react too well."

Emmett chuckled, his mouth curving into a grin. "According to your father, you threatened to take the money Grams left to you and disappear. South America, was it? Maybe it was New Zealand?"

Recalling the argument, one of many Wyatt had with his father, he felt his face flush. "Montenegro. I read about it in my world history class. It sounded cool." He shrugged, still unclear about how he'd decided on the small country in Europe. "What can I say? At eighteen, I saw myself as a man who could make my own decisions. Pop telling me where I'd live and work while attending Montana State didn't work for me."

"Yet here you are, eight years later, with a dual degree in Ranch Management and Facilities Management, and a wealth of experience in operating a dude ranch. Quite an accomplishment while putting in twenty hours a week here. Your aunt and I have often wondered if you lost out on the activities at the campus by living here."

"I did as much as I wanted. Football games, a few dances. I also competed on the Bobcat rodeo team for three years."

"And did real well. You've also spent a good deal of time marketing our dude ranch. The last few years have been our best, Wyatt."

The two men fell silent, watching the fire while lost in their own thoughts. Leaving tomorrow would be bittersweet. Wyatt loved living and working with his aunt and uncle. He wished the two family ranches were closer so they could visit often. Two hundred plus miles wasn't a huge distance. When you're responsible for dozens of animals and providing work for no less than twenty men, time shared with extended family was rare and precious.

"I'll be back, Uncle Emmett. The drive isn't that long. Don't forget, I can still work on promoting the dude ranch from home."

"Assuming your father lets you have the time. My sense is he's more than ready for you to return to Whistle Rock Ranch."

"Don't worry about my time. I'll find extra hours to work on marketing. You have great internet access here, and ours is pretty good. We'll be able to do whatever we need via our computers."

Wyatt placed a hand on Emmett's shoulder when his uncle didn't look too convinced. "You'll have to trust me. I will always make time for you and Aunt Lucinda."

Emmett and Lucinda were like second parents. They'd tried for years to have children of their own without success. When Wyatt asked them why they hadn't adopted, his aunt had looked away, not meeting Emmett's gaze. He'd later learned Lucinda begged her husband to consider adoption, but he refused to even discuss the option. Wyatt had never asked the reason.

Seeing Lucinda approach, he opened his arms. Neither said anything for several long moments, although Wyatt could feel his aunt shaking with tears she wouldn't want him to see. After a while, she pulled away.

"You'd better keep in touch, young man. If not, I'll come looking for you."

Chuckling, Wyatt kissed her cheek, emotion close to controlling him. Leaving would be harder than he imagined.

"You can't fool me, Aunt Lucinda. I'm betting it won't take long for you to tire of my emails and calls."

She slapped a palm against his chest. "You're a rascal, Wyatt Bonner. You know I'll never tire of talking with you." Stepping away, she took a moment to control the emotions raging through her.

Lucinda had known this day would come. When he'd first arrived, eight years seemed forever. Now that it was over, she realized it had been a flash in time. Wyatt had become the son they couldn't have. Lucinda felt the loss wrap around her heart, squeezing until she could barely breathe.

Feeling an arm snake around her waist, she leaned into her husband's side. "We'd best let the boy get to bed, sweetheart. He plans to leave before sunrise."

Sunrise, Lucinda thought. Then Wyatt would be gone.

Wyatt gripped the steering wheel tighter than necessary, concentrating on the road ahead. He could see the storm coming, knowing there wasn't a chance he'd outrun it.

His aunt and uncle had been on his mind since driving away from their ranch. Lucinda hadn't been able to stop the tears, and to Wyatt's surprise, Emmett swiped at a few on his face as well. Wyatt hadn't lingered, afraid he'd join them if he didn't get on the road.

Wyatt would miss them, the same as he'd missed his parents and two younger brothers when leaving eight years earlier. Yes, he'd returned to Whistle Rock Ranch a couple times each year. Staying more than a few days wasn't possible with school and the nonstop work at Gallatin Dude Ranch.

His father, Anson, couldn't be more different than Emmett. Both were smart, knew ranching better than most. That's where the similarities ended.

Where his uncle had a way of encouraging his ranch hands with encouraging words and examples, Anson used the threat of firing to get what he wanted. The biggest lesson Wyatt learned over eight years was his uncle's way resulted in much better results.

Lightning up ahead drew his attention back to the road. Traffic was light, and visibility good. Glancing at the clock, he'd been driving for almost three hours, making good time. From the flakes landing on his windshield, that would change soon.

Within minutes, the light snow grew to storm level, reducing how far he could see ahead. He knew the road well, having driven it for years. It didn't mean much in a storm such as the one slamming into his truck.

Checking the rearview mirror, his jaw clenched. The horse trailer had begun to weave, inching closer than he liked to the edge of the road. He recalled the drop off to be a steep three feet. If the truck and trailer went over, Mighty Quinn wouldn't survive. Wyatt guessed his chances would be less than twenty percent.

Gripping the steering wheel, he increased his speed. Within seconds, the trailer straightened out, following on a straight line behind the truck.

Leaning forward, he blinked a few times, concentrating on what he could see. Wiping sweaty palms on his Wranglers, he groaned at the sound of his phone. With visibility deteriorating, he let the call go to voicemail.

Tightening his grip on the steering wheel, he checked the rearview mirror, realizing he could no longer see the trailer. Sucking in a deep breath, he let it out on a slow whoosh, feeling his heart calm.

It had been a long time since he'd driven in a storm as wicked as this one. Releasing one hand, he flexed his fingers. Doing the same with his other hand, he stared ahead, not quite believing what he'd seen. Headlights gleamed in the distance.

Heart pounding, Wyatt didn't allow himself to relax. Glancing in the mirror once more, he let out a breath. The white trailer carrying his prized Mighty Quinn came into view.

Returning his gaze to the road ahead, he whooped in relief. As if an answer to his prayers, he left the gray of the storm behind to enter a sky as deep a blue as any he'd ever seen.

Chapter Two

Wyatt parked at the top of the ridge, gazing out at his favorite sight. From here, he could see the entire ranch to the Grand Tetons across the valley.

The ranch house, barn, and bunkhouse were all painted red, the same as when his parents first built them over thirty years earlier. Wyatt knew how long it took to repaint each one.

The Paint horses his family bred and trained grazed in a pasture to the far left. He guessed there to be about twenty. They were what made Whistle Rock Ranch well-known in the United States and abroad. The pride and joy of Anson and Margie Bonner.

The last tugged down the corners of Wyatt's mouth. He sometimes felt the precious Paints, as his mother called them, were valued more than the couple's three sons. Dismissing the dismal thought, he grabbed the small cooler filled with food Aunt Lucinda had given him before leaving.

Pulling out a roast beef sandwich, Wyatt ate while continuing to scan the ranch. His father had mentioned during a phone call a new building had been erected not far from the bunkhouse. He saw no evidence of it, nor did he recall what the building would be used for. Still, he noticed quite a few changes.

Finishing the last bite of his sandwich, he chugged a bottle of water, tossing it in the back seat of the truck.

"You're stalling, Bonner." Speaking the words out loud made them real.

Wyatt knew when he left it wasn't about the miles between the two ranches. His father had sent him on a journey to discover his future, decide what he wanted from life.

He'd known when his parents waved goodbye there'd been more to their decision to send him to live with his aunt and uncle than experiencing life on another ranch. They were sending him a message.

Unlike many oldest sons on nearby ranches, Wyatt enjoyed every minute of life. He played sports, attended dances, dated, and pranked with the best of them. He also tackled all the chores his parents gave him, and did a darn good job.

Along the way, he somehow achieved grades high enough to be accepted to Montana State University, and accepted on the school's prestigious rodeo team. From Wyatt's view, life was great and getting better.

Graduation day had been one big party. He'd had a great time, staying up until almost sunup. Crashing on his bed, Wyatt had anticipated sleeping in until noon.

Instead, his father had woken him at eight, ordered Wyatt to get showered and dressed, then set a large plate of eggs, bacon, and potatoes in front of him. Something about the way his father leaned against the doorjamb, arms crossed, had warned Wyatt his life was about to change.

At four o'clock that afternoon, he'd maneuvered his truck and horse trailer to the front of his aunt and uncle's house. By six, the new plan had been spread out before him.

Years later, he sat in the same truck, with the same trailer behind him, studying the ranch below. Yes, the ranch showed changes, but he'd changed too.

Eight years, and this cowboy had begun the long road home.

"There he is, Anson." Margie Bonner, hair and nails freshly done, set aside the ledger and stood.

Placing the Stetson on his thinning, gray hair, Anson met his wife at the front door. "Took the boy long enough."

"Don't you start on him. He's been gone too long already. I don't want him to turn around and head back to Montana." Margie turned to give her husband a warning look. "I'm serious, Anson."

Frustration creased his brow. "We discussed this already."

"And I'm reminding you we decided to give Wyatt time to adjust before you start barking orders at him."

Bending down, he kissed her temple. "You're right. I'll give the boy time."

Margie watched her oldest boy, so tall and handsome, get out of the truck he'd bought before leaving for Emmett's. "We'd best get outside."

Not waiting for Anson's reply, she rushed out the door toward the son who stood waiting, his arms open wide. Slowing in front of him, she stepped into his embrace.

"It's so good to have you home, Wyatt."

"I've missed you, Mama." He glanced up to see his father approach, the familiar sour expression creasing his face. Kissing his mother on the cheek, he stepped to the side, holding out his hand.

"Pop."

Anson looked down at the outstretched arm, sighed, then took it. "Wyatt. You had a good trip?"

"Yes, sir. A storm came through, but nothing I couldn't handle."

Dropping Wyatt's hand, Anson walked past the truck to the back of the trailer. "Mighty Quinn is ready to touch solid ground. You best get him out of there."

Wincing, Wyatt shot a pained glance at his mother before joining his father. Without a word, he opened the back door to climb inside with Quinn. Stroking his horse's neck and withers, he spoke to the Paint gelding in a soothing voice.

"I'll bet you're ready to get out of this jail, boy." Connecting the lead rope to the halter, he guided Quinn out of the trailer.

"He'll be in the same stall as before. Jonah and Gage's horses are still here."

Wyatt's younger brothers attended the University of Wyoming in Laramie. Jonah would graduate in June with an MBA and law degree. Gage would also graduate with a bachelor's in outdoor recreation and tourism. Wyatt had never asked his father, or his brothers, why neither of them were expected to work at their uncle's ranch.

Walking his gelding into the cavernous barn, he stopped. All stalls, including the one Mighty Quinn used, were full.

"Forgot you don't know about the family barn. That's where we put our own horses." Anson stood in the shadows, his arm extended. "It's behind the bunkhouse."

Wyatt knew that was one of the new buildings he'd seen from the stop where he ate lunch. "I saw it, and some other new buildings, from the turnout. Figured you'd explain when we had time."

Following Anson out the back door, he led Quinn to a smaller barn. There were eight stalls, three more than needed for the family.

"What do you think?" Anson stood next to him, arms crossed as his gaze moved around the building.

"It's nice, Pop. Did you lay it out?"

"Me and Virgil."

Wyatt's face lit up at the mention of his best friend, Virgil Redstar. He'd returned to the ranch three years earlier, after obtaining a pre-veterinarian degree from the University of Wyoming. He'd hoped to become a vet, but there'd been no money for tuition. Wyatt was still angry at his father for reneging on his offer to pay it if Virgil received his bachelor's degree. He suspected Virgil's father, Jasper, the ranch foreman, was behind Anson's change of heart.

"Is Virgil at the ranch today?"

"He's somewhere around. Jasper would know."

"Which is Quinn's stall?"

"To the right of Jonah's horse, Winston."

On a nod, Wyatt walked Quinn to the side door, removing the lead rope. "I'm going to put him outside for a while. Do you mind if I go find Virgil?"

Anson wanted to go over his plans for the ranch, deciding to put it off until that night. "Jasper is with the men in the far left pasture. If Virgil isn't with him, Jasper will know where he is."

"Thanks. I won't be gone long."

"Better not be. Your mother is expecting you at the house. She's having Nacho cook a big spread for tonight. Some kind of welcome home meal. Don't disappoint her." Turning on his heel, Anson headed out the front, leaving Wyatt to wonder what had caused the man's sour mood.

He didn't linger on it long. Anson Bonner was known for swift mood changes, from foul to charming. Wyatt couldn't keep up when he was younger, and doubted a few years away would make a difference. His father was driven to be the premier breeder and trainer of registered Paint horses in the world.

Wyatt couldn't argue with anyone else's dreams. The problem he faced was figuring out his own.

The Paints were a wonderful breed. They were magnificent at everything, and were born with a perfect temperament. Whether working around the ranch or competing, he couldn't identify a better overall breed.

Gage had selected a Morgan as his own horse. Wyatt couldn't argue with his choice. Theodore had served his brother well. The one disadvantage was the gelding's stature. At over six-feet tall, Gage should have a horse over sixteen hands. Winston was fifteen-three hands, above average for a Morgan.

Jonah preferred his registered quarter horse, Winston. Similar in many ways to Gage's Morgan, his gelding was fifteen-three hands. Jonah and Gage were about the same height, meaning each should be riding a horse over sixteen hands.

Wyatt didn't care if their chosen horses made sense. All three brothers loved their geldings.

Watching Mighty Quinn run in a large circle in the pasture, throwing his head back and snorting, Wyatt couldn't hold back a laugh. At least his horse was glad to be home.

His feelings were less decisive. He loved seeing his mother, and looked forward to catching up with Virgil. Thoughts on his father were less clear.

Always a robust man with endless energy, Anson's skin appeared pale, and he seemed more exhausted than normal for early in the afternoon. He'd also lost weight.

Wyatt guessed him to be at least twenty-five pounds lighter than during his last visit.

Jogging away from the barn toward the far pasture, he waved at several ranch hands. He spotted two new storage sheds behind the original barn, as well as a new round pen used for training.

Crossing one of the many ranch roads on the property, a grin appeared. Virgil Redstar stood next to his father, watching as a ranch hand worked with one of their Paints.

The last email from Virgil mentioned training a couple of the men to work with the Paints in order to fulfill orders more quickly. Wyatt knew the man in the ring, remembered him to be even-tempered, with plenty of patience and a light touch. A man Wyatt would've chosen himself.

His hopes of surprising Virgil died when one of the hands raised a hand in greeting, calling his name.

"Wyatt. It's good to see you." Jeramy Barrel, one of the longtime Bonner hands, walked toward him. "Hey, man. Heard you might arrive today." Tugging Wyatt into a bro-hug, he laughed. "It's real good to have you back."

"It's good to be home." It wasn't a lie, and wasn't the exact truth. He hoped to figure the difference out soon. "Are you one of the men Virgil is working with?"

Jeramy threw back his head to laugh again. "Heck no. Virgil says the energy flowing off me would scare them Paints. I work with the other breeds. The ones not so attuned to my moods. Virgil's words, not mine. I'd better get back over there. Jasper Redstar is on a terror today. Don't want to anger my boss." Slapping Wyatt on the back, he jogged back to the group, passing Virgil.

"It's good you're here, Wyatt." Virgil stopped in front of him, watching the smile on his friend's face grow.

"Can't get along without me, huh?" Before Virgil could answer, Wyatt pulled him into a hug. "Missed you, you ole Cheyenne." Dropping his arms, he took a step back.

"You, too, white man."

Both laughed at the familiar greeting, which had begun when they were in elementary school. They'd both been sent to the principal for a talk about respect. Leaving the office, Virgil had slung an arm over Wyatt's shoulders.

"Let's play basketball, white man."

Laughing, Wyatt had slung his arm around Virgil. "Sounds good to me, you ole Cheyenne."

The ritual still felt good all these years later.

Chapter Three

"A heart attack? Why didn't anyone call me?" Wyatt felt his face heat, anger forming in his chest.

"Your father forbade anyone telling you, Jonah, or Gage. Your mother backed him up, and so did my father."

"To be expected. Whatever my father says goes. What happened?"

"Anson was out riding with my father and a few ranch hands. They were rounding up stray cattle on the north side of the property. Something set Anson off, and he began yelling at one of the men. My father said he grasped his chest, growled like a bear, and fell to the ground. One of the men called 9-1-1, then Margie, while another rode back to the compound to guide the EMTs to their location."

"Where were you?" Wyatt knew all about Virgil's medical training. Besides a degree in pre-veterinary science, his friend had considered EMT training.

"On my way back to town. The ranch truck was loaded with supplies. Something didn't feel right when the ambulance passed, so I took off after it."

"You were lucky one of Garth's men didn't pull you over."

"A deputy would've if they'd been anywhere around. I followed the ambulance out to where Anson was on the ground. All the ranch hands know basic first aid and CPR. They did what they could. It helped since Anson was still alive when the EMTs arrived."

Scrubbing a hand down his face, Wyatt stared past his friend to the group of men working the Paints. "When?"

"Three months."

Throwing up his hands, he paced away. Wyatt needed a few minutes to cool off so he wouldn't storm into the house and say something he'd regret. No wonder his father appeared pale, and tired easily. The man had suffered a heart attack, and not thought it important to tell his sons.

Feeling a hand on his shoulder, he knew Virgil stood beside him. "Your parents didn't want to interfere with your studies. There wasn't anything you, Jonah, or Gage could've done. Anson required rest, and a great deal of it. My father and I were here to keep the ranch going."

"How long was he in the hospital?"

"Three weeks." Virgil chuckled as he recalled the ruckus Anson had caused several times in the final days. "They were happy to see your old man leave."

"My father has the same effect on a lot of people. How long has he been out of bed?" Wyatt still had a hard time believing his father had a major heart attack and no one notified him. Especially Virgil.

They were tight. Best friends since elementary school. Did Virgil believe Anson would fire him if he notified Wyatt of what happened?

Rubbing his temple, he had to accept his father would fire his own mother if she went against a direct order. Anson knew no other way to handle people. The man would never change.

Shifting toward the sound reminding him of a sewing machine on steroids, a smile broke across his face. He could hear a country western song blaring out the open windows, and see her mouth move with the words.

"Who in the world is that?"

Virgil followed his gaze to see a familiar red VW bug bump along the road. A cute blonde behind the wheel. "She's boarding her horse here. Comes out three times a week, sometimes four, to ride her."

"Since when did we start boarding horses to outsiders?"

Casting Wyatt a sympathetic look, Virgil chuckled. "She's a local. You must remember her. You dated her a few times before graduating."

The smile fell from Wyatt's face. "I don't remember a red VW."

"Daisy bought her in Laramie while attending the University of Wyoming. She drives it or the red GMC SUV her mother gave her as a graduation present."

"Daisy?" His jaw dropped. "Crazy Daisy Raines?"

"You'd better not call her that now, brother. She may have been a little quirky in high school, but she owns a business and does real well. Besides, I taught her how to protect herself. She's a spitfire."

Wyatt watched as she parked, waving at some of the hands as she got out and started for the barn. "Protect herself?"

"A drunk attacked her last summer when she left her shop. According to the deputy who responded, Daisy's scream was louder than an emergency siren. The woman has lungs."

Wyatt didn't care about her lungs. "Was she hurt?"

"A few bruises, and a cut above her eye. She was more scared than anything else. So I offered to give her some lessons in self-defense. Daisy's a fast learner."

Pulling his attention away from where she disappeared into the barn, he looked at Virgil. "I don't remember you knowing her that well."

"She attended U of W when I did. Daisy, Jonah, and I would get together for lunch, dinner, or a concert sometimes. She's a year younger than us. A year older than Jonah. We attended her graduation last May."

"You say she already has a successful business downtown?" From what Wyatt remembered, Daisy couldn't talk on the phone and write down an address at the same time. Virgil had to be mistaken about running a shop.

"Artsy stuff, the same as her degree. Daisy paints, makes jewelry, and is a terrific photographer. A lot of local artists place their work in her shop. She does special events that draw in people. One Saturday each month, she invites kids between five to sixteen to paint for the cost of materials. I stopped by once. Daisy was great with the children."

Virgil didn't mention Daisy was best friends with his former girlfriend, Lily Cardoza. They'd gone out for over two years before he graduated and left for Laramie. His father had pushed him to break up with her. A decision Virgil still regretted. Lily barely spoke to him eight years later.

"Maybe her kind of crazy appeals to kids." Wyatt winced at the unkind words.

"I'll remind you one more time. Don't call her crazy. To her face or behind her back." Virgil shot him a serious look before walking a straight line to the barn.

"Hey, wait up." Jogging, he caught up with Virgil. "Sorry, man. You're right. I promise not to use the word crazy in relation to Daisy ever again. Scout's honor."

"You weren't a scout."

"Oh. Right."

The barn was empty by the time they entered. "She's already in the corral."

"What horse did she purchase?" Wyatt wondered if she'd gone for a Paint or one of the other breeds.

"Honey."

"Mom sold Honey? That's not possible."

Virgil stopped, pointing outside to the corral. "Look."

It took Wyatt's eyes a moment to adjust enough to recognize the ten-year-old mare his mother had hand fed as a foal. Daisy had already slipped a halter over Honey's head, attached the lead rope, and was speaking to the horse while stroking her nose.

"Daisy's real good with her."

"Does she ride alone?"

"I go with her sometimes. Lily rides out with her other times, and one of the ranch hands selects a ride for her. Margie has gone a few times." When Wyatt didn't respond, Virgil looked at him. "What?"

"The same Lily you broke up with after graduation?"

"One and the same. She doesn't speak to me. That's why I have her work with one of the hands. Better for both of us."

"It's been eight years. I'd think she'd be over it."

Virgil always felt a pang of regret recalling the afternoon he'd broken up with Lily. The night before, they'd talked of their future, how they'd get their degrees, marry, and wait a few years for children. Both had been committed to the other and a shared life. A few hours later, he'd blown their plans, and their love, apart without a word of explanation.

"I deserve her scorn, Wyatt." He didn't explain further. Instead, Virgil nodded toward the corral. "Here comes Daisy. Are you going to stay or run?"

Blowing out a snort, he shot his friend an incredulous look. "What makes you think I'd run?"

"Perhaps the way your hands are stuffed in your pockets. You do that when you're uncomfortable."

Immediately removing them, he crossed his arms. "I'm not going anywhere."

Chuckling, Virgil shook his head as Daisy approached. "Good afternoon."

"Hey, Virgil." Tilting her head, she squinted at the man next to him. "It can't be. That isn't the mysterious Wyatt Bonner next to you, is it?"

"Funny." Wyatt stepped aside to let her and Honey enter the barn. "Good to see you, Daisy."

Stopping in front of him, she looked up. "You got taller."

"Nah. You shrunk."

The cute straw hat on her head tipped when laughter burst from her lips. "I'll have you know I grew half an inch after graduating."

Leading Honey to a wall full of saddles with blankets folded on top, she selected hers. Placing the blanket over Honey's back, she smoothed it while talking to the mare. Easily lifting the saddle, she centered it, careful to make sure the mare wasn't holding in air before cinching it tight.

Exchanging the halter for the bridle, she again spoke to the horse before turning toward the men. "Either of you up for a ride?"

Her bright smile slammed into Wyatt's gut. She was too darn cute, with long, blonde hair pulled into a ponytail, freckles splattered across her makeup-free face, and blue overalls over a long sleeved, white t-shirt.

Dangling from her ears were white and yellow...well...he wasn't certain what they were. Hearts maybe. Or flowers?

"I'll ride along." Wyatt winced, unsure why he'd offered.

Daisy watched the play of emotions on his face with amusement. "Are you sure? You look a little green."

"Of course I'm certain." Although he wasn't, and he didn't understand why. Which wasn't true. Wyatt did know why he should let her go without him. Daisy Raines, with her quirky ways and airy personality, would never fit into his world.

"Because I'm fine riding by myself."

Placing fisted hands on his waist, his mouth twisted into a grimace. "I said I'm certain. I'll saddle Mighty Quinn and we'll be on our way."

A sound behind him had Wyatt whirling around. Virgil stood beside Mighty Quinn, the gelding already tacked up and ready to go. He handed over the reins to Wyatt, turned around, and left the barn without a word to either of them.

Jaw tight, he led the gelding outside and swung into the saddle as if he'd been born to it. Which he had.

Turning, he stared at her. "You coming?"

Daisy rushed to mount Honey and join Wyatt outside. "All set."

"Anywhere in particular you want to go?"

"As a matter of fact, I planned to ride to Whistle Rock."

Leaning back, he wondered if she really might be crazy. "That's an hour ride up and back."

"Yep." She clucked, signaling Honey to start walking.

"At least two hours in total."

"Aren't you the smart one. An hour plus another hour does add up to two." She continued toward the trail as Wyatt came up beside her.

"It'll be pushing dark by the time we get back. You sure you want to be gone so long?"

"I'm certain. There are a few pictures I want to take for a new project. The light will be perfect for my needs by the time we stop at the rock." She turned toward him, the same irritating smile still plastered on her face. "Don't feel you have to go with me." She clucked again, sending Honey into a jog.

Wyatt let her ride ahead, trying to understand why his stubborn streak always showed up around Daisy. He'd never understood her effect on him. Not in high school, and not eight years later.

Moving Quinn into a jog, he gave up trying to figure it out. He'd take this one ride with her and be done with it. One ride, and she'd fade back into her quirky life, allowing him to deal with the serious problems of running a ranch.

Chapter Four

"Heard you went for a ride with Daisy Raines this afternoon. Didn't you date her in high school?" Anson rested in the leather recliner tucked into a corner of his large office, his piercing eyes pinned on his oldest son.

Wyatt knew his father wouldn't be able to stay away from the topic of Daisy. Anson hadn't been a fan of his son dating her in high school, and Wyatt doubted the elder Bonner's doubts about her had changed.

He found it interesting. Wyatt couldn't quite decipher his own feelings about the somewhat eccentric woman, yet his father's doubts brought out his protective instincts.

"We went out a few times. Nothing serious." He rubbed his chin, deciding how much he wanted to say. "Daisy came to the ranch today to take pictures for a commission. The client wants a large watercolor of Whistle Rock, with the Tetons in the background. It's a significant deal for her."

"Your mother's a huge supporter of Daisy's. We have one of her watercolors in our bedroom. Doesn't mean I'm behind her efforts to lobby the Brilliance city council for money."

"Money?"

"For more public art projects. We have enough statues, mosaics, and murals already. There are a lot of people who don't see how the money helps our local economy."

The argument was an old one Wyatt had heard many times. "Tourists like the artwork, Pop. They see what's been done as enhancing Brilliance."

"That young woman uses the projects to promote her own work. It's a scam, nothing more."

"It's a store, Pop. She offers lessons, as well as showcases art from locals."

"From what I've seen, most of what's in the shop is her own work." Anson held up a hand when Wyatt opened his mouth to protest. "Her store isn't why I want to talk to you about Daisy."

Warning bells chimed in his head. Wyatt didn't want to go through another discussion of why a woman wasn't good enough for the Bonners' oldest son. The reasons couldn't be any different from what he'd heard in the past.

He'd never been serious about a woman. Nothing close to how Virgil felt about Lily.

"Pop, I don't need a lecture about getting serious with Daisy or any other woman. When I find the right one, I'll be the one to decide whether or not she's good enough for me. You might as well save your breath for a more important topic, such as your heart attack."

Anson's face flushed, his hands balling into fists. "Who told you?"

"It's not important. Everyone knows about you being in the hospital. Everyone except your three sons. We had a right to know, Pop. Why did you keep it from us?"

"Have you told Jonah and Gage?"

"Not yet, but don't think I won't. I want to know what was going through your mind to decide we shouldn't be told."

Relaxing, Anson's head fell back against the chair, his eyes closing. He said nothing for so long, Wyatt thought he'd fallen asleep.

"You were all in school. I didn't want my medical issues impacting your studies. May not make sense to you, but the decision was mine, and I'd do it again."

"Mom went along with it?" He could see by the change in his father's face his mother had fought the decision.

"She went along with it. Don't go thinking any less of her for supporting me. Margie is the best woman I've ever known. She's the type of woman I want for my boys. Daisy isn't that type of woman, Wyatt. I believe you've already figured that out."

"I haven't figured anything out about Daisy. She may be different than any of us without ranch experience. Still, she's a good woman with a big heart. Doesn't make her any less than us."

"She's no rancher's wife."

"Never said she was."

"Then it'd be best to stay away from her. No sense getting her hopes up, son."

"Pop, I respect your opinions. The thing is, I'm old enough to make my own decisions about women, and most everything else. You try telling me what to do and we're going to have problems."

"As long as you're living in this house, you'll do what I say." Anson's voice rose with each word, along with the color in his face.

"Calm down, Pop."

"Don't tell me to calm down." Lowering the chair, he started to rise.

Raising his hands, Wyatt took a few steps forward. "Maybe you should stay down for a bit."

"What's going on in here?" Margie stormed in, walking straight to her husband. "You stay where you are." She whirled on Wyatt. "What did you say to him?"

"What am I ever able to say that doesn't set him off? And why didn't you tell your sons about his heart attack?"

The steam seemed to go out of her at his question. She looked tired and defeated. "Your father wouldn't allow it."

"And I won't allow you to see that Daisy woman. You do, and you're out of this house."

"Anson, that is quite enough. Wyatt, why don't you go on to the living room. Everyone's gathering for supper." She looked at her husband. "Including that Daisy woman. And you darn well better be nice to her."

"I'm not a monster, Margie." The wind seemed to have left his lungs, his color changing from red to a yellowish pallor. "Get me out of this chair."

"I'll help you, Pop."

His mother held up her hand. "No. You go on and say hello to your friends, Wyatt. I can help your father."

"If you're sure?"

Closing the distance between them, she placed a kiss on his cheek. "I'm sure. Please, go on now."

Staring at his father for a few seconds, he did as his mother asked, not at all happy with how
the conversation had ended.

The house couldn't hold one more person. Most everyone who lived and worked at the ranch were inside, along with several of his friends from school, and a few friends of his parents.

Wyatt spotted Virgil in a corner, holding a bottled soda in his hand, talking with one of the ranch hands. Daisy and Lily stood a few feet away, the latter with her back to Virgil.

He hadn't seen Lily since high school. She was even more beautiful than he remembered. It must be killing Virgil to be so close to her and know she had no use of him.

Wyatt's gaze moved to Daisy. Something Lily said made her laugh, and the sight hit him in the chest. He wondered how she looked when angry or sad, because in all the time he'd known her, he'd never seen her without a smile. Not even the day he'd said goodbye. She'd kissed his cheek and wished him the best.

Wyatt had told her he'd stay in touch. He never had. Not an email, text, or phone call. He'd driven away and forgotten all about Daisy Raines. Watching her now, he wasn't sure how he'd done it, or if he could do it now.

He didn't have to date her to know she was sunshine in a world of gray skies. Aunt Lucinda was the same. Her bright personality drew people to her, making her someone people wanted to call a friend. Daisy had the same effect on those who met her. Wyatt found himself wanting to be her friend.

"Hey there, stranger."

The voice had him turning, already knowing who stood behind him. "Vivi."

A smile curved his lips as his arms wrapped around her, whirling her in a circle. Setting her down, his gaze wandered over her. "You look amazing."

"So do you, cowboy."

"What are you doing here? The last I heard, you were living in London."

"Still am. I needed some time back home. Mom and Dad aren't getting any younger, and my younger brother is, well...he's not making life easy for anyone."

Taking her hand, he tugged her toward a corner where there were two empty easy chairs. Sitting down, he leaned toward the woman who'd become a good friend in junior high and high school.

They'd met at thirteen in study hall, becoming fast friends. She and Virgil were the only people outside his family he stayed connected to while in Bozeman.

"Tell me what's going on."

"This is a celebration, not a pity party, Wyatt."

"Tell me, Vivi."

"You already know my parents are older. Mom is in her late seventies, and Dad is a year older. She's never been in the best of health. Dad can handle her issues fine. It's my brother who's making things hard. You remember, he's six years younger than me. He graduates this year. The sheriff or his deputies have picked him up several times in the last few months. Nothing serious, but each call weighs on my parents."

"Have you talked to him since coming home?"

"Not yet. He's camping with friends."

Wyatt's brow lifted, his mouth twisting. "In this weather? There's a minimum of two feet of snow down here. It was deeper at Whistle Rock."

The only reason he and Daisy made it up there today was the county kept the short trail plowed for visitors to the local landmark. By mid-December, the trail would be closed until late March.

"I know. That's what Dad told me. The truth is, I don't know where he is."

"I'll talk to him, Vivi. He's always listened to me."

Standing, she leaned down, wrapping her arms around him. "Thank you, Wyatt. I'd hoped you'd speak with him."

Shoving up, he kept an arm around her. "All you had to do was ask. We're still the same friends we used to be. Right?"

"Right."

"I'm starving. Let's get something to eat."

Across the room, Daisy watched Wyatt and Vivi. She'd always known they were tight, the same as Wyatt and Virgil. The same as her and Lily.

"Hey, how long do you want to stay?" Lily bit down on another of the delicious cream cheese and parmesan mini crescent rolls. "I mean, the food is incredible, and it's free."

Daisy laughed, knowing what her friend meant. "Does that mean you'd prefer to stay a little longer?"

"Sure. I don't want to cook dinner when I can graze on all this. Plus, the ranch hands aren't hard to look at."

Smiling, Daisy grabbed one of the mini crescents. "These *are* good. Someday, I'll learn to make appetizers as good as these. Did you have any of the antipasto kebobs? They're incredible."

She finger waved at Virgil, who stood across the table. His gaze had followed Lily since she'd arrived for the party. Daisy felt bad for both of them, knowing each still loved the other. For different reasons, neither would make the first move.

Virgil responded with a chin lift before turning to the woman who'd come up next to him. She watched as they spoke for a few minutes before Virgil dipped his head and left the woman standing alone.

"You know Daisy, right, Vivi?" Wyatt's deep voice had her whirling around, wondering how they'd come up without her noticing.

"Of course. How are you, Daisy? I've heard your shop is doing great." Vivi gave her a quick hug.

"I'm doing great, Vivi. You look fabulous. How's London?"

"As you'd expect. Cold, exotic, crowded. I do love my job, though. The man is quite eccentric, and demanding. Underneath it all, he has a huge heart."

"You're his executive assistant?" Daisy took another crescent roll, taking a bite.

"Private secretary is what he prefers to call me."

Wyatt watched the two women with interest. Both beautiful, upbeat, with a gleam in their eyes signaling their positive attitudes. The same, yet different.

One was a best friend. No matter how he'd tried, Wyatt had never felt anything except friendship for Vivi.

Then there was Daisy. He didn't know how he felt about the perky, hardworking artist and shop owner. A woman who drove a red VW bug.

God save him from people he might never understand. Even so, he felt a tiny tug toward her. A tug he didn't understand, yet was determined to explore.

Chapter Five

Wyatt sat atop the cutting horse he'd been training in the indoor arena, using subtle signals and the gelding's own instincts to get what he wanted. The Paint had been born at Whistle Rock Ranch, shown for four years before Virgil began serious cutter training.

Virgil handed the gelding over to Wyatt so he could work with another gelding. Both were being trained for the same buyer, a man who had more money than sense when it came to the serious work of cutters.

Besides training the horses, the ranch had to keep a solid herd of cattle. These were used just for their cutting horses. Nothing about the process was cheap.

Both Virgil and Wyatt had been competing since they were fourteen, progressing quickly from local events to regional competitions. Along with cutting, they participated in high school rodeo, both winning a fair share of events.

College put an end to their cutting competitions, but not rodeo. Each found a place on their respective teams, competing against each other on a few occasions. Virgil stayed on the University of Wyoming team for four years, Wyatt on the Montana State team for three, before work at his uncle's dude ranch required his time.

At twenty-seven years old, they focused on whatever was needed at Whistle Rock Ranch. Right now, it was preparing the two geldings to compete in cutting events.

Two weeks had passed since Wyatt and Daisy had ridden to Whistle Rock. Not a day went by he didn't think of her. Wyatt fought the irritation of having her pop into his head at the strangest times. The images always showed her laughing or smiling, the way she'd been the entire day, and during the evening celebration.

He'd watched her during his welcome home party, wishing some of her constant happiness would rub off on him. Not that he had a bad life. Far from it.

Living with his father's harsh moods wore on him. Uncle Emmett had been different. It took a rare situation for him to lose his good humor. Problems were challenges to work through, not obstacles met with severe words and actions. Some of Daisy's upbeat nature would sure help during those times.

Since a boy, Wyatt had handled his father's outbursts by drawing into himself while getting out of Anson's way. Living on a ranch had made the last easy. There were always chores to complete, many a good distance from his father.

It hadn't been Wyatt's choice to live and work on Uncle Emmett's ranch while attending college. The experience had ended up better than he ever could've imagined. He'd mentioned to Virgil it would be good for Anson to stay at the dude ranch for a few months. Maybe the time there would mellow him out a little.

"You done with him for now, boss?"

Sliding to the ground, Wyatt handed the reins to the nearby ranch hand. "Cool him down, then put him out. He did good today." Removing his hat, he swiped moisture from his forehead. Even the cold weather couldn't keep him from working up a sweat.

"Will do."

Tired and thirsty, Wyatt grabbed his jacket off a hook and headed toward the kitchen's back door. Mid-afternoon would find Nacho, their cook for the last ten years, preparing supper for whichever Bonners were on the ranch, plus Jasper, Virgil, and any guests. He found himself hoping for a quiet meal.

"Hey, Nacho. What's for leftovers?" Wyatt had asked the same everyday after school. Grabbing two water bottles, he finished one in a few seconds before removing the top from the second. Setting it aside, he opened the refrigerator to peer inside.

"Wash your hands before touching anything, mano."

Wyatt moved to the sink. "You've gotten grouchy over the years, old man."

Nacho continued cutting vegetables for supper, ignoring the comment. "I heard you and Anson had an argument last night."

Removing a plate of leftover roast beef from the refrigerator, he chewed on a slice. "Wasn't an argument. We disagreed about him not telling me, Jonah, and Gage about the heart attack."

"He had his reasons." Nacho exchanged the sliced carrots for a bag of onions.

"Yeah? Well, I have mine for wanting to know. You all still see us as kids. We aren't. Keeping that from us was wrong."

Glancing up from where he held a knife with a lethal edge, Nacho gave a slow nod of understanding. "Your father won't change with age."

"And Mother will always support him."

"Yes, she will."

Grabbing another slice of cold beef, he chewed while considering what to do. He believed Jonah and Gage should know about the heart attack. What did their father think they'd do? Freak out about it?

Jonah was ready to enter the dual MBA/law degree program. He was quiet, bright, and levelheaded. Little ruffled him. Gage might be the daredevil of the three, taking chances his brothers wouldn't, but he didn't do anything without thorough research. Calm and gentle, he would take the news well.

"Don't do it, mano."

Wyatt whipped his head to look at Nacho. "What?"

"Tell your brothers without letting Anson know first. It might send him back to the hospital."

"What if they swore to not say anything?"

The knife stilled, Nacho lifting his face to meet Wyatt's gaze. "Has that worked in the past?"

"Sometimes."

"It's not worth the risk."

Nacho was right. He usually was when it came to Wyatt's parents.

"Make a sandwich and get out of my kitchen. I have work to do."

Chuckling, Wyatt did as Nacho said, taking a huge bite of a ham and beef sandwich as he headed back outside. A familiar red VW bug sat parked near the large barn. It's owner, dressed in skintight jeans, a thick emerald green sweater, and unbuttoned, heavy coat, held a camera in both hands. Following where it pointed, he spotted his mother leaning against one of several tractors.

Deciding to keep his distance and watch, he smiled at the way Daisy directed his mother to move a little to the right, tilt her head, smile. Checking the image, she had Margie shift positions again and lift her chin. Over the fifteen minutes he stood watching, Wyatt guessed Daisy took at least thirty shots.

"You just going to stand there all day? Don't you have chores to do?"

Deciding to ignore the grumpy tone of his father's voice, he nodded toward the women. "Why's Daisy taking so many pictures?"

"Some foolish idea about putting together a calendar of local ranch women. Your mother is going to be January, with the snow and all." Taking a few steps to stand beside his son, Anson stared at his wife. "She's still the prettiest thing I've ever seen." His voice had softened, holding a wistfulness Wyatt had never heard.

"You all right, Pop?"

The question had the effect of a cold bucket of water tossed over Anson. "I'm as fine as ever." The gruffness had returned, as well as the sour expression.

"Is Daisy trying to get the calendar ready to sell for next year?"

"Heck if I know, but makes sense. Your mother is the last woman she needs to complete the calendar."

"It's early November. Guess that's enough time to get it printed and put up for sale."

"Doesn't matter to me. What I care about is the men standing around watching. You'd better get them moving before I fire the lot of them."

"Sure thing, Pop." Wyatt jogged toward the group of men, not wanting their interest in the photo shoot to provoke his father. "Time to get back to your chores."

"We've got to wait here a bit longer, Wyatt."

Planting his boots shoulder width apart, he crossed his arms. "Why's that, Barrel?"

A smile broke across the short, barrel-chested ranch hand. "Daisy wants us to be in the calendar with your mother."

"She does?"

"I do. If you're willing, I'd love to have you in it too." Daisy held up her camera, showing Wyatt the last shot. "The one I'm doing with your mother and ranch hands will be at the back of the calendar. You could stand right next to her, with Virgil on the other side."

Dropping his arms, Wyatt's brows drew together in confusion. "Virgil's going to be in it?"

"Why, yes." Daisy turned toward the group of men. "How about you all get in front of the barn." Spotting Virgil, she waved, motioning him to join the others. "Go head, Wyatt. You and Virgil both being in the shot will blow up the interest."

"And why's that?"

"Are you kidding? Two handsome, hunky cowboys standing next to your gorgeous mother? Plus, you've got a whole group of men working here women will love to gawk at."

Grabbing his arm, Daisy hauled him along with her to the front of the barn. "Right there, next to your mother."

She took several minutes moving men around before coming up with a configuration she liked. Virgil stood on one side of Margie, Wyatt on the other. All three grinning. Standing back, Daisy let her gaze take in the entire group. Satisfied, she lifted the camera.

"Everyone look at me. One...two...three." She snapped several pictures, shouted a few requests, then took a few more. "That's it. Thank you all for agreeing to be in the calendar."

Wyatt broke from the group first. "All right, men. You heard the lady. Time to get back to work." He turned around in time to see Barrel speaking with Daisy.

"Thanks for including us, ma'am. I'm going to buy ten of those calendars for my family." Touching the brim of his hat, the ranch hand returned to his work.

"Can I see the last shots?"

Daisy lifted her head from her perusal of the shots before handing the camera to Wyatt. "I think one of the last two would be best for the calendar."

"They're both good. The second to the last is a little better." He handed the camera back. "At least in my opinion."

"You've got a good eye, cowboy."

"Two of them."

She chuckled, her stomach doing flips at how close Wyatt stood beside her. "Yeah. Two of them. Well, I should get back to the shop. I've hired a junior at the high school to help out, but he has band practice at four, so I'd better head out."

"What are you doing for supper?" He blinked at the question, unsure as to why he'd asked. If his father found out, it would mean another argument.

By the look on Daisy's face, his question stunned her too. "I was going to warm up a pizza."

"How about I pick you up at six-thirty and we'll go to that new place at the end of town?"

Her stomach muscles danced at the invitation. She'd had a crush on him since high school, been ecstatic when he'd taken her out a few times at the end of her junior year. Daisy knew it would end when he left for college, but the memories remained through the last eight years.

"I'd like that."

"Great. I'll see you in a couple hours." Walking Daisy to her car, he waited until she turned around and made it to the road.

Feeling good, he turned to lock gazes on the outraged glare of his father.

Chapter Six

Wyatt didn't allow himself to be drawn into a discussion with his father. Anson had already made his feelings clear on Daisy. He loved and respected his father, which didn't mean he'd let the man manipulate him, or try to run his life.

Turning on his heel, Wyatt headed in the opposite direction from where his father stood near the house. Walking toward the barn, he shoved any doubts about having supper with Daisy aside.

No, she wasn't the kind of woman who normally attracted his attention—tall, slender, and most significant, born and raised on a ranch. Those women were often too intense for his taste.

Wyatt had enough issues to deal with during the day. In the evening, when he had time to leave the ranch, he wanted light and fun. A woman who'd make him relax and laugh.

At twenty-seven, he had plenty of time to fall in love. His father was in his thirties before marrying his mother. Wyatt would have to remind his father of that the next time he said anything against Daisy.

Laughter near one of the corrals caught his attention. Following the voices, he found Virgil talking to an older couple, and a woman who appeared to be in her late teens. Seeing Wyatt approach, Virgil waved him over.

"This is Wyatt Bonner. Wyatt, Mr. and Mrs. Chafin, and their daughter, Deidre. They're interested in purchasing three of our Paints." Virgil shot him a meaningful look the two had perfected since they were kids, which conveyed their visitors had little or no experience with horses.

Wyatt stuck out his hand. "It's a pleasure to meet you."

Mr. Chafin clasped the offered hand. "You're just the man we came here to see."

"Is that so?"

"The man at the western wear store said to ask for Mr. Bonner."

"Ah. He probably meant my father, Anson."

"No, it was you," the man insisted. "He told us your father was recovering from a heart attack, and you were acting in his place."

Wyatt felt pretty sure his father wouldn't want to hear his son was taking his place. Or to know those in town were talking about his medical issues.

"I see. Virgil and I handle the Paint breeding program. Why don't we sit down and you can tell us about your experience, and we'll explain how we work."

Wyatt led them to an office at one end of the large barn while Virgil held back, answering Deidre's questions. The girl appeared enamored of his Northern Cheyenne friend, her eyes wide as she hung on his every word.

Virgil had always attracted women, old and young, with his long, black hair, caramel brown eyes, and golden, light brown skin. His broad smile and easy manner didn't hurt, either.

Thirty minutes passed as Wyatt and Virgil went through their list of questions while answering those the Chafins asked. It didn't take long to learn Virgil was right about their skill level. Neither of the parents had more than a few hours on a horse.

In contrast, Deidre had spent several summers living on a horse ranch back east. She'd become proficient at hunt seat riding and dressage, even participating in horse shows.

"Are you certain you want a Paint, Deidre?" Virgil asked. "We breed, train, and sell thoroughbreds, also."

"I read about the ranch before we came out. It said Paints, quarter horses, and thoroughbreds are your specialty." She glanced at her parents, then back at Virgil. "I'm ready for a change to a Paint. And I want to ride western, and learn barrel racing and breakaway roping."

Virgil sat back in his chair, releasing a burst of air. "You can't get much different than dressage and barrel racing. They both use distinct equipment and riding skills. You'll be starting over."

Wyatt leaned forward, resting his arms on his legs. "Is there a reason for the change?"

Deidre shrugged, looking again toward her parents. They looked as confused as Virgil and Wyatt.

"I never really liked dressage. While the other students watched videos on English riding, I'd watch the Cowboy Channel. To me…" Deidre shifted in her chair, as if uncomfortable with what she was about to confess. "It's exciting, and more physical. Do you teach barrel racing?"

Wyatt sat up, rubbing his jaw. "What about Jaycee Hendricks or Patty Moore, Virgil? Are they still around?"

"Both are here. I know Jaycee is teaching. Not sure about Patty." He looked at the Chafins. "Both are state and regional champions. Jaycee won second at the NFR about eight years ago. I'd start with her since I know she's still coaching."

"Will she come here, and can I ride my own horse?" Deidre asked.

"Yes to both." Virgil pulled out his phone. "I'll call to make sure before we look at the horses."

Wyatt pulled out a notebook while Virgil made the call. "These are the Paints ready for sale. I believe we have six to choose from. However, we have a dozen more we can finish training and have ready in a few weeks. Keep in mind we're at the very early stages of winter. All of you will train in our indoor arena, including Deidre. We plow our large corrals, but they're for our use, not for students."

"You do help match a horse to each of us, right?" Mrs. Chafin had spoken little since arriving at the ranch. If Wyatt wasn't mistaken, she hadn't committed a hundred percent to taking up riding.

"Yes. Matching riders and horses is required."

"You mean, I can't choose my own horse?" Deidre's disappointment was obvious.

"It's a joint effort." Virgil slid the notebook between him and Deidre. "Do you prefer a mare or gelding?"

"I've been riding a gelding the last two years. I'm open to buying a mare. What do you suggest?"

"I'd like to see you ride two different horses before making a decision." He opened the book, pointing to one of the horses. "This is Gaucho. He's five, and tops out right at fifteen hands. We've just begun training him for cutting, although I believe he'd be an excellent mount for barrel racing. What do you think, Wyatt?"

"I haven't spent much time with him. How about we see if Jaycee is willing to come out and give us her opinion?"

Virgil nodded, turning to another page. "Good idea. We'll have her look at Gaucho and June Bug. She's also five, with some training and show experience. She's fourteen-three hands, so a little smaller. How tall are you, Deidre?"

"Um, five-four." Taller was better in the world of English riders. She didn't believe it mattered as much for barrel racing.

"Perfect for either horse." Closing the book, he spoke to Wyatt. "Let's get them outside to look at the horses before it gets too dark."

Wyatt put the wipers on high before increasing the heat inside the truck. He'd gotten a late start for his six-thirty date with Daisy. *Date.* He couldn't remember the last time he'd taken a woman out for a meal, or even something as simple as taking a trail ride.

Studying for dual degrees while working on the dude ranch had taken all his time. He'd taken the occasional walk with one of the female clients his age, but those weren't dates or romantic. They'd been nice breaks in his busy schedule.

Noting the storm had passed, he turned off the wipers, keeping the heat on high. His mind moved to Daisy. Wyatt didn't know why he'd asked her to dinner when he wasn't certain he even liked her. Well, yes, he did like her.

She was interesting, upbeat, and they always parted with him feeling great. So different than the way he felt around his parents. His mother had long ago given up her earlier role of peacekeeper between her husband and their sons.

By the time Wyatt entered high school, Margie Bonner had made the decision to be firmly behind her husband, no matter her own beliefs. It had been a hard lesson for all three Bonner boys. The mother they idolized decided to let them handle their own disagreements with their father.

At sixteen and fourteen, Wyatt and Jonah accepted their mother's decision, taking on the challenge of dealing with their controlling father. At ten, Gage didn't understand his mother's defection.

The three Bonner brothers did love their mother, the same as they loved their father. The love for their parents was tempered compared to how it had been when they were younger.

Wyatt parked in front of Wind Song, Daisy's shop. A few lights were still on and he could see her standing near the back. Even alone, a smile shown on her face.

Climbing out of his truck, he ignored the Closed sign to join her inside.

"Hey, Wyatt. You're right on time."

"This is a great place you have, Daisy."

She came around the counter, stopping a few feet away. "That's right. You're a first timer."

Chuckling, he picked up an exquisite glass bowl. Holding it up, he marveled at the swirls of red, green, and purple.

"This is amazing."

"Bobby Burns and I were in school together. He's a very talented glass artist. All of the work in my shop is by Wyoming artists."

"I know you paint pastels and watercolors. Virgil told me you also create jewelry. Which of the pieces are yours?"

An enchanting blush crept up Daisy's neck to her cheeks. "Well, the jewelry in the glass counter is mine." She walked back to where she'd been when Wyatt arrived. "I use gold, silver, and semi-precious stones. No two are exactly alike."

Unlocking the case, she pulled out a pair of earrings. "These have become a favorite. I've made over a hundred pairs since the shop opened, although each one is different."

Taking them from her outstretched hand, his eyes widened at the intricacies of the metal work, and stunning stones. "Incredible. You're very talented."

Chuckling, she took the earrings back. "How would you know?"

"My Aunt Lucinda makes jewelry, which is sold in galleries in Montana, Wyoming, Idaho, and the Dakotas. As you know, I lived with her and my Uncle Emmett for the last eight years. There were times I helped her in the studio."

"Lucinda? Oh, my goodness. Lulu Bonner. She's your aunt? I never put it together with the Bonner ranching families. Her work is fabulous. I'd love to meet her someday."

"Then you will. Which are your watercolors?"

"The wall behind you is all me. Watercolors and pastels."

"All of these?" He walked closer, marveling at the range of colors and subjects.

"Most all are landscapes. Lately, I've been dabbling in people."

"Wait a minute." He bent down, getting a good look at a smaller canvas. "Is that Virgil?"

"It is. What do you think?"

"It's great." His voice had turned almost reverent. "You captured his smile perfectly." Straightening, he looked at her. "Has he seen it?"

She shook her head. "You're the first. I put it up after closing the shop tonight."

"Excellent. I want it."

"Really?" Excitement poured from that one work.

"Yep." Reaching into his pocket, he pulled out a handful of bills. "But I want to leave it here until his birthday."

"I'm not going to talk you out of it. That has to be the fastest sale I've ever made."

His face sobered as he looked back over his shoulder at the pastel of his closest friend. "You captured him better than a photograph, Daisy. You have a real gift."

Handing him the receipt, her smile slipped. "Thank you, Wyatt. It means a lot coming from you."

Chapter Seven

Daisy's comment stayed with Wyatt through dinner and on his drive back home. He didn't know why. She possessed an amazing talent for an artist in her early twenties. Yet she seemed genuinely shocked, and grateful, at his praise.

Entering the house, Wyatt saw the light underneath the door of his father's office. Not interested in ruining what had been a wonderful evening by encountering his father, he headed for the stairs.

"We need to talk."

Shoulders slumping, Wyatt turned to see his father standing in the office doorway. The color of his skin and defeated stance made Anson look years older than he appeared earlier in the day.

"It's been a long day, Pop. Can it wait until tomorrow?"

Taking a moment to answer, his father shook his head. "No. It can't."

"All right." It wasn't late, yet exhaustion nagged at Wyatt. A confrontation with his father over Daisy might put him over the edge, allowing him to say something he'd later regret.

"Sit down, son." Instead of taking the chair behind his desk, Anson lowered himself onto the leather sofa.

Wyatt chose the seat nearby. "You look tired, Pop."

"No more than usual."

The response surprised him. His father had always shown boundless energy, could work twelve hours outside, then another six in his office before joining Margie in their bedroom. The heart attack had taken more out of him than Wyatt knew.

"Did you have a good time tonight?"

The question surprised Wyatt. There wasn't a hint of disapproval in his father's voice.

"Yes. She's put a lot of work into her shop. Daisy is quite talented."

"So your mother says."

"She painted a pastel of Virgil. It's an amazing likeness. I bought it for his birthday."

Tapping fingers on the arm of his chair, Anson stared straight ahead.

"What did you want to talk about?"

"I'm going to hand the reins of the ranch over to you, Wyatt."

Dumbfounded, his entire body stilled, wondering if he'd heard his father right.

"I see I've surprised you."

Leaning forward, he rested his arms on his thighs, locking his intense gaze on his father. "I don't understand."

"It's simple. The heart attack took a lot out of me." Anson stared down at his lap before lifting his head to meet Wyatt's concerned gaze. "Margie had been nagging me to cut back before the attack. Now she's all over me about my diet, blood pressure, rest. And passing along most of my work to you."

Sitting back, Wyatt drew in a slow breath, taking in his father's words. Several minutes passed before he could wrap his mind around the changes Anson proposed for Whistle Rock Ranch.

"I'm not ready."

"You've been ready for years."

Wyatt shook his head. "I know nothing about the ranch accounting."

"I'll be handling the books. Eventually, you'll be taking them over. You already know our banker, CPA, and attorney. We'll be meeting with them together from now on."

Rising, Wyatt paced to the small refrigerator hidden within the custom cabinets. Removing a bottle of water, he drank half of it before recapping it.

"Tell me what's going on, Pop. You're not as weak as you want me to believe." Retaking his seat, Wyatt waited, determined not to leave before hearing his father's explanation.

Shrugging, Anson clasped his hands together. "I'm sixty-two years old. My father started this ranch, and the same as you, he had me working since my tenth birthday."

"I'm not sure feeding the horses and filling water troughs count."

"Chores are important, and you always pulled your weight. Jonah and Gage love the ranch, although it's different with them. Jonah will return to handle the legal issues and business contracts. Gage…" Anson let out a breath. "I'm not sure what that boy will do."

"Once Gage graduates, we'll be able to offer guide services. Fishing, hunting, hiking, and camping programs. Those are his passions." Wyatt swallowed more water, a knowing grin curving his lips. "We might as well exploit them."

"He also wants to become a smoke jumper. Your mother won't be happy if he does. Which brings me to the real reason for my decision. Margie has stood by me through some mighty tough times. Many you know about. Some you don't. She's loyal and completely devoted to our marriage. Even when standing by me put a wedge between her and you three boys."

Staring at the floor, Wyatt thought of all the times his mother had disappointed her sons by supporting their father. "I understand."

"It's time I took that woman on the vacation we've put off for over thirty years." Standing, Anson opened a desk drawer, pulling out a stack of brochures. Dropping them on the table next to Wyatt, he sat back down. "I'm thinking a cruise."

Wyatt didn't know how he'd been able to hold back a laugh when his father mentioned a cruise. He couldn't see the man who'd raised him standing in buffet lines, lying by the pool, or playing bingo with a table of blue-haired ladies.

Withholding his less than supportive comments, he'd scooped up the stack of brochures, carrying them upstairs to his bedroom. An hour passed as he read about the variety of activities and shore excursions.

Texas Hold'em, private restaurants, country music, and movie nights would appeal to his father. No doubt his mother would sign up for dance and cooking classes. The land activities were numerous and varied. Deep sea fishing would appeal to both his parents.

Locking his hands behind his head, Wyatt stared at the wood plank ceiling. It had been a night of revelations. The extent of Daisy's talent and business skills surprised him. She may come across as flighty to some, but anyone with eyes could see she was smart, determined, and dedicated to making her shop a success.

Entering the house, he'd wanted nothing more than to disappear into his bedroom and think about his evening with Daisy. His mind now centered on how in the world he could take over for his father.

Though gruff and often difficult, Anson was the heart and soul of the ranch. He had a unique persona, which couldn't be passed onto a successor.

His father was right about Wyatt having the skills to manage the daily operations. The men would listen to him. Even Virgil's father, Jasper, would follow his orders. The rest would come with time.

Casting a look at his phone, Wyatt had the strangest urge to call Daisy. He wanted to share the meeting with his father and ask her thoughts. This type of call would more often be between him and Virgil. Why Daisy came to mind baffled him. They may have grabbed burgers a couple times in high school, shared a ride to Whistle Rock, and eaten Italian food tonight, but the woman wasn't close to being a good friend.

Jonah and Gage were who he should call. Wyatt wanted to hear their reactions to their father's announcement, discover if they had any objections. Both would return to the ranch at some point. Jonah after obtaining his law degree and MBA, Gage after finishing his undergrad degree.

Their return wouldn't change anything except add more knowledge and ideas about how to grow the ranch. Virgil would also have a place in the decision making. Jonah and Gage respected him, often deferred to him in matters regarding their training programs.

Reaching for his phone, Wyatt tapped in Daisy's number. Hovering over the call button, he again rethought why the first call would go to her and not Virgil or his brothers.

Too tired to consider the reasons or anything else, he cancelled the call and closed his eyes. Tomorrow would be soon enough to confront the questions plaguing him tonight.

Daisy rushed around the shop, adding new pieces and rearranging displays before opening for the day. She'd accepted a new pottery artist a few days earlier, as well as a bronze sculptor who specialized in smaller pieces. Their work should arrive soon.

Each month exceeded the previous one, her profits rising beyond projections. Jewelry, small, framed paintings, and pottery flew out of the shop. If the same pieces were purchased in Jackson Hole, they'd be at least thirty percent higher. Visitors willing to drive a few more miles found treasures at prices set to encourage the purchase of several pieces.

The strategy worked well. She'd need to seek a larger space, or possibly build a loft if the growth continued. There was no reason to believe it wouldn't.

Finishing, she unlocked the front door, welcoming a man and woman inside. "Let me know if I can answer any questions. There's a great deal to see, much of it new."

Keeping watch on the customers, her mind went to the night before and her date with Wyatt. They'd fallen into comfortable conversation, as if eight years hadn't past. It had been the same during their horseback ride to Whistle Rock.

She hadn't been on a date in a long time. Part due to long hours in the shop, and part because of the lack of men who interested her. Then there was the third part—a lack of invitations.

Since moving back after graduating from college, she'd had a total of three men asking to take her out. Two were townsfolk, an accountant and the owner of an office supply store. The third worked on a ranch about forty miles away. The first two were reserved, making it hard to hold a normal conversation. At least a conversation she enjoyed.

The cowboy was funny, outgoing, telling outrageous stories. When the evening ended, he acknowledged forty miles was a little far to date, especially in the unpredictable weather of Wyoming. He had wanted to stay friends and leave the door open to call her in the future.

She'd been disappointed, but thankful they'd gotten to know each other. He'd called a few times to catch up without inviting her out.

Wyatt asking her to dinner had been a complete surprise. Wonderful and exciting. She'd fretted about it since leaving the ranch, second-guessing herself on what to wear. A rarity for her. As the time grew closer for Wyatt to arrive, she'd decided the clothes she wore would have to do.

Their time together had been wonderful, yet Daisy knew better than to expect much from him. Margie liked her well enough, even calling to meet for coffee or lunch. She was a huge supporter of the shop, and arts in general. Such a contrast to her husband.

Anson didn't hide his dislike for Daisy, which puzzled her. They'd spent little time together, having perhaps three short conversations consisting of a couple sentences. She never asked Margie about it, not wanting to create tension between the older couple.

She wondered if Anson knew Wyatt had asked her out. If so, Daisy would've loved to have heard their conversation.

"We want to purchase this as a gift. Do you wrap?" The woman held out a bracelet Daisy had finished and placed on display the day before.

"I'd be happy to wrap it for you. What's the occasion?"

"Her birthday's in a week. This bracelet is perfect. And so beautiful."

"Thank you. It's been in the shop less than two days." Daisy took the bracelet from the woman's outstretched hand.

Eyes wide, a grin spread across the woman's face. "Are you the artist?"

"I am."

"Well, you are extremely talented." Digging into her purse, the woman handed her a card. "We own a gift shop in Jackson Hole. Let me know if you're ever interested in showing your work."

Taking the card, Daisy read the information. "Thank you. I'll give it some thought."

Tucking it into a pocket, she already knew her work would be exclusive to Wind Song, the store she'd dreamed about since a teenager.

It was one of two dreams she'd kept close to her heart. The first, a place to display her work. And second, a dream she'd voiced to no one else. She wanted Wyatt Bonner to fall in love with her.

Chapter Eight

Wyatt tugged up his collar while keeping watch on the darkening sky. He'd been riding the fence line since minutes after sunrise, racing to round up any stray horses before the building storm let loose with Wyoming force.

The projections called for three feet of snow in twelve hours, with more to follow. A real doozy is what Nacho warned as Wyatt raced out the kitchen door with an egg sandwich clamped between his teeth and a thermos of coffee tucked under an arm.

Virgil and most of the ranch hands were driving the horses to pastures closer to the compound. Most were already in safe territory. Soon, all their prized stock would be secure.

Continuing his search for stray horses, he thought of the night before. He hadn't been able to wrap his mind around his father's decision to slow down. Wyatt understood it could take months to recover from a heart attack. Some people never did get back to a hundred percent. Maybe his father was one of them.

Hearing the neigh of nearby horses, Wyatt reined Mighty Quinn around. The gelding had a sixth sense when it came to locating cattle or horses. Uncle Emmett said Quinn had cattle instincts, a critical trait of any cutting horse. By anyone's standards, his Paint gelding was one of the best.

It didn't take long to locate a group of four horses bunched together where the north and west fence lines merged. Giving Quinn his head, the gelding took less than a minute to round up the four and push them toward the new pasture.

Wyatt loved this part of ranching. The freedom of riding in the open, just him and Quinn. If it wasn't a necessity, the cell phone in his pocket would be back in his bedroom. As if reading his thoughts, the phone rang. Keeping watch on the tiny herd, he tugged it from his pocket.

"Hey, Virg."

"We've got all the horses in the pasture. We're missing four."

"Quinn and I are bringing them in."

"That's what I hoped to hear. Where are you?"

"Riding back from the far northwest pasture. About thirty minutes out."

"I'm on my way."

Chuckling, Wyatt slid the phone away. So much for peace and quiet.

To be honest, he thrived on the structured chaos of ranch life. His father had taught his sons well, making them work alongside the ranch hands. They mucked stalls, cleaned chicken coops, and washed down the birthing stalls, all while being educated by the best.

His father now wanted to back away, vacation with his wife, and pass the torch to his sons. The fact Wyatt would be taking on the bulk of the management responsibilities didn't scare him. What bothered him was the niggling sensation there was more to his father's decision than slowing down.

The black duster caught his attention first as Virgil approached. Wyatt let out an ear-piercing yell, smiling when his best friend returned it.

"We've got everything buttoned down at the ranch." Virgil's attention moved to the storm moving swiftly over the ranch. "The sky's going to open up any minute." His prediction came true thirty seconds later.

The snow slowed their progress, taking them another twenty minutes to reach the gate. Virgil released it, waiting as Wyatt herded the four horses inside. Closing and locking the gate, Virgil reined his black and white Paint mare, Migisi, toward the ranch.

Wyatt tugged his hat lower on his forehead. "Let's get into the bunkhouse before we freeze to death."

"Then you can tell me what inspired you to go out on your own with this storm threatening."

"It was a foolish decision."

"Yes, it was. One of your worst ideas." Virgil closed the door to the two bedroom foreman's apartment at one end of the bunkhouse, where he and his father lived. Shirking off his heavy coat, he started a fire before adjusting the thermostat.

"Mind if I make coffee?" Wyatt didn't wait for a response as he filled the water reservoir. It had been his present to Jasper on his last birthday.

"The new coffeemaker has grown on him. Kicked and screamed like a little girl when I unplugged the old one and tossed it in the trash. But he came around." Virgil handed Wyatt a canister filled with coffee pods. "It's good for him to make changes."

"Change comes slower as we get older."

Crossing his arms, Virgil leaned against the counter, one brow lifted. "What's going on?"

"Pop is handing the day-to-day responsibilities to me."

Shoving away from the counter, Virgil took a seat next to him. "You're not joking?"

"Nope. He plans to take Mom on the vacations they didn't take since starting the ranch. I'll manage the ranch work while he'll continue with the accounting. We'll be meeting with the banker, CPA, and lawyer soon. We're going to talk sometime today." Standing, he set his cup of coffee aside and started one for Virgil. "I believe there's more to his decision."

"You think there's a medical reason?"

"Maybe. I can't ask Pop." Picking up his cup, he returned to the table, grabbing an apple from a bowl of fruit. "Since when do you keep apples, grapes, and oranges around?"

"Since the doctor told him he needed to eat more fruit."

"I don't know if I'm ready."

Sipping his coffee, Virgil pinned Wyatt with a hard look. "You're ready."

"There's still so much to learn."

"Do you think Anson knew everything when he took over from your granddad? We both know he didn't. He'll still be around, so will my father, and I'm here. You're going to do fine. Better than fine. You need to speak with your mother."

Pushing the chair away, Wyatt walked into the kitchen, tossing the apple core into the trash. "I know. It's doubtful she'll tell me much."

"Ask. She might surprise you."

The entire building shook.

Taking a step away from the counter, a gale force gust slammed into the side of the building, knocking him backward. Seconds later, another blast hit, this one breaking the glass in two windows.

Grabbing his coat, Wyatt slipped into it before stepping to the door.

"Don't go out there. The storm needs to pass before we check the damages." Virgil stood to the side of the broken windows, chancing a look outside. "Get over here, Wyatt. Tell me what you think."

Standing on the other side of the open window, Wyatt ran fingers through his hair, his mind racing. "I don't recall seeing anything like this. You?"

"No. Nothing we can do until it slows down."

Pulling out his phone, Wyatt punched his father's number. When the call went straight to voicemail, he tried his mother, shaking his head when he got the same result.

"The storm must've taken out the service." Putting away the phone, Wyatt hurried to the door leading to the front part of the bunkhouse.

"Where are you going?"

"I have to check on Pop and Mom. Make sure they're all right."

Reaching out, Virgil grabbed Wyatt's arm, pulling him back. "You aren't going out there until the storm passes. There's zero visibility. You could get lost and freeze to death."

"What if Pop needs help?"

"The big house has a backup generator system, several fireplaces, and enough food for months."

Wyatt thought of the satellite phone they used when the weather or lack of cell service made communication impossible. He should've taken one with him that morning. The same with Virgil.

"Where's Jasper?"

Jaw tight, Virgil shook his head. "I don't know."

A loud knock on the door leading to the large bunkhouse was followed by Barrel's booming voice. "Virgil. You in there?"

Reaching past Wyatt, he drew the door open. "What is it?"

"It's Jasper." Barrel nodded behind him. "We finished breakfast and started playing cards until the storm lifted."

Virgil shoved past him, barely hearing Barrel's next words. "He's not breathing too well."

Hurrying to the far end of the building, Virgil spotted his father at a table, face flushed as he fought to breathe. Sliding a chair close, he faced Jasper.

"What's going on?"

Working to suck in a breath, his father shook his head.

"Does anyone have a sat phone?"

Barrel shook his head. "Unless you have one, they're all at the main house."

Hearing Barrel's comment, Wyatt joined Virgil. "We need to get him to the hospital."

"Not...going."

Sharing a meaningful look, Wyatt headed to the nearest window. "The storm's slowing down. I'm headed to the house. Get Jasper ready to leave."

"I'll go with you." Barrel buttoned his coat and slammed a hat down on his head before grabbing gloves. "Let's go."

"Stay close," Wyatt shouted over his shoulder as he hurried through the fresh snow toward the house.

The lights shone through the windows, indicating the generator was doing its job or the power had come back on. His father stood behind a window, watching Wyatt and Barrel's progress.

The front door swung open as they hit the porch. Stomping their boots before entering, both men stopped a few feet inside. Margie stood next to Anson, one arm through his.

Unphased by his parents' unusual show of affection, Wyatt rushed his explanation. "Jasper's having trouble breathing. We need to get him to the hospital."

Lifting the sat phone from its holster, Anson called 9-1-1. "We have an emergency at Whistle Rock Ranch. One of my men is having trouble breathing. Yes, I know about the storm and power outage. I need an ambulance out here now. Not in an hour or two."

Anson felt a hand on his arm and looked down to see Margie's painted fingernails pressing into his skin. Taking a breath, he listened to the woman on the other end of the line.

"Fine. We'll get him to the hospital. Yes, I know the danger. Well, since you won't send help, it's up to us to get this man to town. Lady, I don't know how long you've lived here, but we're three generation ranchers. We've been taking care of ourselves long before you were born." Ending the call, Anson looked at Barrel.

"Get the SUV in front of the bunkhouse. There should be plenty of gas. Wyatt, go with your mother to get blankets, water, and two sat phones while I get my jacket and boots."

"You are not going with them, Anson Bonner." Margie stood in front of him, arms crossed, blocking his path. "Wyatt, Barrel, and Virgil will go, but you're staying here."

"She's right, Pop. The three of us will get Jasper to the hospital. Virgil will drive. He knows all the alternative routes if some of the roads are closed. Mom? Can we get the blankets and water?"

"And sat phones." Anson forced his attention to his son. "They're charged."

Returning with a bag filled with water bottles, several blankets under his arm, and the phones tucked into his pockets, he headed past his father to the door. It opened, Barrel motioning him.

"Jasper's loaded. Let's get out of here while there's a lull in the storm."

Handing the blankets and waters to Barrel, Wyatt turned back to his parents. "I'll call when we get there. Don't worry. Jasper will be back here in no time."

Chapter Nine

Virgil sat with his head in his hands. They'd reached the hospital without incident. Within minutes of the emergency workers wheeling his father inside, Barrel parked the SUV just as another storm let loose. All the three men could do now was wait. Something none of them had much talent at.

Standing, Virgil stretched his arms above his head. "I'm getting coffee. You two want some?"

"I'll get it," Wyatt offered.

"I need to walk around a bit. Be back in a few minutes." Scanning the waiting area without seeing a place to buy coffee, he walked to the nurse's station. "Where can I get coffee?"

"Oh, I'm sorry. Our machine broke and we're waiting for a replacement. If you go through the door to your left, you'll find another one down the hall."

"Thank you." Entering the hall and closing the door, the silence enveloped him.

The waiting area had a surprising number of people, including young children and crying babies. Virgil could tell the area didn't see many people other than hospital staff. Leaning against a wall, he scrubbed both hands over his face.

His father turned fifty-four on his last birthday. Fit and mentally sharp, Virgil couldn't recall the last time Jasper had been ill. Watching him struggle to breathe, not knowing how to help him, scared Virgil more than he'd admit. Not since his mother walked out on them right after his fifth birthday had he experienced such acute pain in his chest.

"Virgil? Are you all right?"

The soft, concerned voice reminded him of one other time he'd felt the same sharp stab to his chest. Lily Cardoza, the young woman he'd dated his last two years in high school. He'd fallen in love with one look. His chest squeezed as it always did when he thought about or saw her. Virgil had been a fool to walk away from her when he'd left for college.

"Virgil, please. What's wrong?"

Opening his eyes, he steeled himself for the impact of his gaze landing on hers. "It's Jasper, Lily."

"He's here?"

"In emergency. He's having a hard time breathing."

"No one's come out to speak with you?"

"Not yet. The coffeemaker out front is broken. The nurse directed me here. Wyatt and Barrel are waiting for me." Pressing his palms against his eyes, Virgil shook his head. "Sorry. I don't mean to ramble."

Touching his arm, she quickly pulled it away at the familiar sensations. It had been eight years, and her reaction to Virgil hadn't changed. "I'll see what I can find out while you get coffee."

Watching her rush off, he felt another stab to his heart. "Lily…"

But she was already gone. The same as when he'd broken up with her after school a few days before graduation. Fighting tears, she'd given one nod of understanding before leaving him alone in the school hallway.

A rushed decision had caused him eight years of regret. Until today, Lily barely spoke to him, didn't acknowledge Virgil unless forced to because of circumstances.

Making three coffees, he headed back to the waiting area. "Sorry it took so long. I needed some time." Handing out the cups, he sat down, wondering what was taking so long.

Staring into the already cooling coffee, he didn't see Lily walk toward them, the hint of a smile on her face. Lifting her chin at Wyatt and Barrel, she stopped in front of Virgil.

"Do you have a minute?"

"It's all right, Lil. You can talk freely."

Stilling for a moment at the use of the nickname only Virgil used, she lowered her voice. "The doctor is talking to Jasper right now. He'll be talking to you soon. I wanted you to know there is a preliminary diagnosis. He's going to order a number of tests, but I can tell you your father is now breathing fine."

Setting down his cup, Virgil stood. "Thank you. I appreciate you coming out here."

"Of course. Well, I'd better get back in there. The doctor should be out soon."

He wanted to reach out, draw her into a hug and never let go. It would take time, but someday, he vowed to have that right again.

"They're going to keep Jasper overnight, Pop. The doctor is pretty sure it's asthma." Wyatt tipped back the bottle of water, swallowing until he'd emptied it. "Virgil is still at the hospital. He'll call when the doctor releases him."

"Asthma?"

"There are still tests to confirm. For now, that's what the doctor believes is going on." Dropping himself into a chair, Wyatt fought off exhaustion from thirty hours without sleep. At seven in the morning, a full day loomed before him.

Leaning forward, Anson rested his arms on the desk, clasping his hands together. "Any idea about treatment?"

"Not until they finish the tests. Virgil is hoping he and Jasper will be home later today, with a plan in place. Asthma isn't a game changer, Pop. Jasper will still be able to perform all his duties as foreman."

Rubbing a hand over his mouth, Anson dipped his head before standing. The storm had passed without further damage. A few broken windows, damage to a round pen, and some other minor issues. Insurance would take care of most of them.

"We have to talk, Wyatt."

"About what?"

"You taking over. I need this to happen soon."

Wyatt heard the urgency in his father's voice. "When do you want to talk?"

"Now."

"Give me a few minutes to get some coffee."

Walking into an empty kitchen occurred so rarely he had to pause and look around. Nacho worked all night preparing meals in case the storm lasted for days. Wyatt figured he could be found asleep in his bedroom behind the kitchen.

Preparing two cups, he headed back to the office. His father stood in the same spot, looking out the window, his shoulders not as squared as they'd once been. When Anson turned to face his son, Wyatt noticed the deep creases around his eyes and mouth. Lines he hadn't noticed a few days earlier.

"Made coffee for you, Pop." He held up the cup.

"Thanks." Accepting the offered cup, Anson lowered himself into one of his large easy chairs. Taking a sip, his lips tilted up. "Perfect."

"Before we start, I have a question for you." Wyatt sat across the large, finely carved coffee table.

"Ask it."

"You've told me what you want me to know about you cutting back. I want to know all of it. The bottom line reason for the change."

A flash of amusement shone in Anson's eyes. "The bottom line?"

"Yes."

"Close the door."

Walking across the room, he closed the door on a soft click before retaking his seat.

"The bottom line is if I don't slow down to what the doctor termed a *crawl*, I won't be around long enough to enjoy my grandkids."

Wyatt sat up straighter. "Grandkids?"

"A figure of speech. If I keep going at the same pace I've kept for close to fifty years, your mother will be widowed within two years. The doctor had the good sense not to say this in front of Margie." Drinking the rest of his coffee, Anson held the cup up. "This will be my last cup of coffee. Doc says I have to switch to tea."

Brows rising, Wyatt leaned toward his father, his heart thumping in worry. "What else aren't you to have?"

"The list is long, and I can tell you right now, I'm not going to stick to it. I might as well be dead if I'm restricted to chicken, fish, and turkey. Chicken and turkey are all right once a month, and fish only if I've caught it. None of the sushi junk you and your brothers like. Makes me gag thinking about putting that stuff in my mouth."

"Doubt you'll have a choice, Pop. Nacho will make what Mom tells him to, and she'll make sure your meals are on the approved list."

"Enough about my diet. Let's talk about you taking on the ranch."

The discussion concluded two hours later, with Wyatt overwhelmed, hoping he could accomplish all his father expected. He knew it could be done when tackling one job at a time.

Wyatt already knew most of what needed managing, having done ranching chores since his tenth birthday. Virgil would have his back, as would Jasper and their ranch hands.

Instead of heading outside to see how the repairs were going, Wyatt walked into the kitchen, ignoring Nacho, who busied himself fixing lunch. Grabbing an apple out of a bowl on the counter, he walked to the bank of windows by the back door.

Watching the activity outside, he allowed himself to think about the one person he hadn't connected with in the last twenty-four hours. He wondered how Daisy and her shop had fared during the storm.

An overwhelming desire to hear her voice, see her, shouldn't have surprised Wyatt. He'd thought of her often since their dinner together. Some may see her as a ditzy blonde whirlwind with brains she didn't use. They'd be dead wrong.

Unlike many people who dreamed, never doing anything to fulfill them, Daisy set goals, made plans, and acted. Wyatt believed he did the same.

She'd returned to Brilliance after college, rented a space within a few days, and opened Wind Song three weeks later. By mid-summer, the store was already making a profit. After sharing the information with Virgil, Daisy would be a great person to discuss his father's decision. Hoping she'd be available for an early breakfast, he pulled out his phone.

Calling her number, he waited until it went to voicemail. Disappointed he couldn't invite her in person, he left a message.

"Hi, Daisy. It's Wyatt. Hope you made it through the storm without damage. If you experienced any problems, let me know. There are some changes going on at the ranch and I'd appreciate getting your input. An early breakfast would be best, assuming that works for you. Call me back when you get a chance."

Pocketing the phone and slipping into his coat, he stepped out into the frigid air. Even with the sun shining, the temperatures were in the high teens. His face stung at the cold.

Loud voices from the other side of the bunkhouse drew his attention. Tugging up the collar of his coat, then pushing down his hat, Wyatt lowered his head, moving toward the group of men.

He stopped when his phone rang. A smile curved his face seeing Daisy's name.

"Hey. How are you doing?"

"Not so good."

The smile fell away as he turned away from the men. Daisy never complained, which worried him. "What's going on?"

"The storm. My shop is..." Instead of finishing, a broken sob told Wyatt this wasn't some frivolous problem.

"Are you at the shop?"

"Yes."

"Stay there. I'm on my way."

Chapter Ten

Rushing toward the men, Wyatt explained what he knew, letting them know he'd bring Virgil and Jasper back to the ranch when the doctor gave his approval. He didn't take the time to let his father know, anxious to get to Daisy.

Wyatt tried to recall the last time he saw her without a smile. Nothing came to mind. The woman never complained or let her personal issues bring others down.

Not even when her father had been diagnosed with cancer. The robust, always pleasant police lieutenant had succumbed to the illness Daisy's sophomore year. She'd held her head high, refused to let the death of the man she loved so much beat her.

Wyatt had seen the truth a week after the funeral. While the other students were in class, he'd rushed to his locker for his calculus book when he spotted a small form sitting alone on the polished cement floor. With her head bent down and hands clasped in her lap, it took him a moment to recognize Daisy. Not wanting to invade her privacy, he hesitated before stepping forward.

"Daisy, are you all right?" Wyatt recalled asking, his chest squeezing when she looked up. Her tear-ravaged face, the painful sob which broke loose, were the answer he'd needed.

The sob he'd heard on the phone today took him back to that day in high school. Whatever happened to her shop had to be serious if it made Daisy Raines cry.

Driving to town in the daylight brought a whole other reality. Trees were down, older fences torn from the ground, porch furniture broken and scattered in yards. The destruction continued into town.

Parking in front of her shop, he stared at the broken front window. Wasting no time, he climbed out of his truck, trying the door. It opened with little effort.

"Daisy?" Looking around, his jaw tightened at the damage. "Daisy, where are you?"

"Here."

Moving toward the voice, he found her sitting on the floor in front of the back counter. Pieces of jewelry were scattered around her. When she lifted her head, he saw the same distraught face as back in high school.

Sitting on the floor beside her, he lifted her onto his lap. He said nothing, just rocked back and forth until she raised her head from his chest to look at him.

Swiping at tears, she blushed. "I'm sorry for being such a wimp."

Using his thumb, Wyatt wiped away another tear. "You've never been a wimp, Daisy."

"This is twice you've caught me feeling sorry for myself."

A chuckle escaped. "Yeah. I remember."

"You do?"

"Of course. You being upset is unusual. That makes it memorable."

Swiping away the last of the tears, she moved out of his arms and stood. "I don't know why this affected me so much. The pieces in the front window are put away at night, so there wasn't much there. The damage is minimal compared to what could've happened."

Standing beside her, he rested fisted hands on his hips and looked around. "It won't take long to put things right. Did you call your insurance agent about the front window?"

"Not yet. I'll do it now."

While she made the call, Wyatt strode to the front. Using his phone, he took pictures of the damage. Putting his phone away, he mentally listed what he'd need to button-up the hole before retrieving a broom and dustpan from the back.

By the time Daisy hung up, he had the front display area cleaned up, as well as the glass on the floor.

"You didn't have to sweep, Wyatt." Her smile had reappeared, letting him know he'd been right to clean up.

"It didn't take long. The damage isn't as extensive as I first thought. What did the insurance agent say?"

"He'll be out in a few hours. Mine isn't the only store damaged in the storm. I can't recall the last time we had such strong winds, along with snow and ice."

"If you'll be here a while, I'll head to the lumberyard to get what's needed to close up the opening." He nodded toward what was left of the front window. "When I'm finished, I'll take you to lunch."

"I don't know. I'm not real hungry."

"You will be by the time I'm finished. It'll do you good to get out of here for a while. Will you be okay here while I'm gone?"

She shot him a cocky grin. "I'm fine. Sorry about my meltdown earlier."

Bending down, he brushed a kiss across her cheek. "No apology needed. I'll be right back."

Daisy watched as he climbed into the truck and drove off. Staring after him, she wondered what possessed her to ask for his help. Priding herself on being self-sufficient, she seldom reached out to others, preferring to do everything on her own.

Wyatt's call had coincided with her little pity party. All would've been fine if she hadn't been crying when he arrived. He must think her a total weakling to let a storm affect her so severely. Of all men to break down in front of, why did it have to be Wyatt Bonner?

Daisy had been in love with the way too handsome and talented rancher since they'd met in junior high. Her father had used his day off to take her to a local rodeo. Wyatt had been competing in the saddle bronc event, taking second place. Not bad for a thirteen-year-old competing against boys of fourteen and fifteen.

A year behind him in school, she'd still spotted him on campus a few times a week. It had been a sad year when he graduated, moving to the brand new high school across town. Joining him a year later, she'd hoped he might notice her. It didn't happen until late her junior year.

Daisy never knew why he'd asked her out. They'd dated for a few short weeks before he graduated and left for his uncle's ranch in southern Montana. She still loved the man eight years later.

"Hey, girl. Looks like you could use some help." Lily Cardoza walked up to Daisy, hugging her best friend. "You should've called me."

"What could you have done, Lil? You were on a twelve-hour shift, and I'm guessing the hospital was busy with the storm."

"You're right. It was crazy. You probably heard about Virgil and Wyatt bringing Jasper in last night."

Eyes wide, she gripped Lily's arm. "I didn't know. What happened?"

"Better. With confidentiality requirements, it'd be best if you asked Virgil for details. So, what can I do?"

"Hello, ladies."

Both women turned to see Wyatt carrying a plywood panel. Setting it down, he returned to his truck, grabbing a couple bags.

Lily leaned toward Daisy. "What's he doing here?"

"Well...he's helping."

Brows lifting, Lily watched as he closed the truck door. "You called him?"

"No. He called me to see how I was doing. When I explained, he drove in from the ranch."

"I'm going to need some help getting the plywood in place." Setting down the bags, he examined the gaping hole.

It took the three of them fifteen minutes to seal the opening and secure the shop. "Lily, I'm taking Daisy to lunch. Why don't you join us?"

"Can't today." She looked at Daisy. "Call me if you need more help. I'm off for two days." Lily left before Daisy could answer.

"Did I say something wrong?"

Righting a picture, she shook her head. "Not at all. Lily's a little sensitive when it comes to anyone who works at Whistle Rock Ranch."

Using the broom to sweep up several more shards of glass, he leaned on the handle. "Because of Virgil?"

"Unfortunately, yes."

"It's been eight years since he left for college." He winced at the words. Virgil still loved Lily, wanted to try again, but the woman wouldn't have anything to do with him.

"I guess eight years isn't long enough for her." It hadn't been enough for Daisy, either.

The difference was Virgil and Lily had fallen in love. She'd thought they had a future together. But when he left for university, he'd ended their relationship. Lily never recovered.

Walking to her, he settled an arm over her shoulders. "Who knows? They could still work things out."

"Doubtful. So, are you going to feed me, cowboy?"

Dropping his arm, he took her hand. "Sure am. I know just the spot."

Wyatt had chosen to sit next to Daisy rather than across the table at Dulcy's Grill. The spot made it easier to hold her hand. She surprised him by not pulling hers away.

"What time is the agent coming by?" Using his thumb, he rubbed circles over her hand.

The look in Wyatt's eyes, the feel of his hand in hers, messed with her mind. He'd never been this attentive during their brief time together in high school.

"Around four o'clock." Swallowing, she tugged her hand from his. "I should look at the menu. There's a lot to choose from."

Hearing the discomfort in her voice, Wyatt set his menu down. "Are you feeling all right, Daisy?"

Her tongue darted out to lick her lips. "Fine. Still a little shaken from the damage to my shop. Other than that, I'm good." It wasn't a complete lie. She was still frustrated about her store. "I'm going to get the bourbon and bacon burger with parmesan fries. And peach pie with ice cream."

Wyatt recalled her appetite was a trait he liked about Daisy. Most women he knew ordered salads with light dressing, or grilled fish with vegetables. Neither with dessert.

"What about you?"

He studied the menu, even though he knew it by heart. "Black and blue burger. Fries and coconut cream pie. No one makes it better."

The waitress set down their drinks, taking their orders before leaving them alone.

"Lily mentioned you and Virgil took Jasper to the hospital."

Setting down his coffee cup, Wyatt let out a breath. "He was having trouble breathing. Turned out, he has asthma. I'm waiting for a call from Virgil to take them back to the ranch."

"Will he able to continue his work at the ranch?"

"I'm counting on it. There's something I wanted to talk to you about, Daisy."

"Sure."

"Pop is turning over the daily operation of the ranch to me."

Her glass of iced tea almost slipped from her hand. "Wow. That's just...well...just, wow." Setting down the glass, she studied his face. "What's wrong?"

Staring into his coffee, Wyatt lifted his eyes to meet hers. "Do you think it's too soon?"

The question startled her. She knew almost nothing about running a ranch. Who she did understand was Wyatt. A leader in everything he tried during high school, Daisy felt certain he'd be a success at anything he tried.

"No."

Brows drawing together, he cocked his head. "No?"

"It's not too soon, Wyatt."

"You sound so certain."

She shrugged, picking up her glass again. "Because I am. Tell me, have you ever failed at anything?"

Snorting out a chuckle, he rubbed the back of his neck. "Sure."

"Okay. Tell me about your biggest failure."

He didn't think long before pinning her with a serious gaze. "Letting you go after graduating from high school."

Chapter Eleven

Instead of surprise or the stunned silence Wyatt expected, Daisy threw back her head and laughed. Her reaction so confused him, his jaw dropped. It took a minute for him to realize she honestly believed he was joking.

"That's good, Wyatt." Swiping at a tear, a smile tilted the corners of her mouth. "What I recall was you couldn't get away from Brilliance or Whistle Rock Ranch fast enough. You probably don't recall, but I was at the ranch when you packed your truck, hooked up the horse trailer, and drove off. You didn't even take time to wave goodbye." Her eyes were still moist from her laughter.

His perception of leaving couldn't be more different than Daisy's. Wyatt remembered it as being exceedingly hard to leave Daisy behind.

Anson gave him no choice. His father and uncle had his life set for the next eight years. He'd attend Montana State University while working and living at Gallatin Dude Ranch. But instead of going back to Whistle Rock Ranch during holidays and summers to see Daisy, he'd stayed on in Bozeman, helping Emmett and Lucinda run the ranch during its busiest season.

Between school, the rodeo team, and working at the dude ranch, time passed without him having any contact with the woman he'd begun to care about. Wyatt made it back to Whistle Rock Ranch for two or three Christmases and one of his mother's birthdays. Other than those brief visits, he'd stayed in Montana, having found he enjoyed life with his aunt and uncle.

Feeling her hand cover his, Daisy offered a smile of understanding. "You are the smartest, most capable man I know. You're going to do a great job managing the ranch. Do you honestly believe your father would pass such a huge responsibility to you unless he knew you'd be a success? All you have to do is believe in yourself."

"Was that what you did when opening your store?"

"That's what everyone must do when they follow their dreams. Is running the ranch your dream or your father's?"

Wyatt had never considered the question. Why would he? He'd always known someday the ranch would pass to him. A born and bred rancher, he couldn't imagine doing anything else.

"Both. I've always hoped to take over for my father. I just never thought it would come so soon."

Leaning toward him, she braced her chin on a hand. "What about Jonah and Gage?"

Crossing his arms, he thought of his two younger brothers. He still needed to discuss their father's announcement with them. "You probably know more about them than I do. I mean, all of you attended U of W."

"Yes, but Jonah is a year younger than me, and Gage is three years younger. I do know Jonah's goal is to earn a law degree and MBA before returning to the ranch. Gage's goals are a little more sketchy."

"An excellent word for my youngest brother. His dream is to be a fishing and hunting guide. Gage also hopes to be accepted as a smoke jumper. The problem with the second goal is jumpers are sent to wherever large fires occur."

Picking up her almost empty glass of water, she took a small sip. "Having a guide at the ranch could work to your advantage. When you and I rode to Whistle Rock, you said your father was considering adding a dude ranch, the same as your uncle. A guide service would be great to offer to your guests."

"Pop hasn't mentioned starting a dude ranch since my return. I know he and Uncle Emmett have discussed it many times. Right now isn't the best time to add something requiring as much attention as a dude ranch."

Daisy nodded at the waitress when she lifted a pitcher of water. Waiting until their glasses were filled, she rubbed a finger around the rim, considering her next words.

"What does starting a dude ranch entail?"

Blowing out a long breath, he suddenly felt tired. "We have some of what is needed already. Trail horses, plenty of tack, a cook used to making meals for large groups. Virgil would make the perfect guide. We'd have to build cabins, prepare marketing material, and design weekly programs. There's usually a last event with music, lots of food, and maybe additional entertainment by the ranch hands or locals. A decision would have to be made about it being adults only or allowing children. Usually ten and older. Some places offer cooking classes on traditional ranch cooking. Other programs offer gourmet classes. It all depends on the interests of the guests."

Thinking about Nacho offering classes had him chuckling. "I'd have to find someone other than Nacho. Someone like you could come in and do a demonstration on making high-end jewelry or painting. Aunt Lucinda would present one for each new group. If it was a week with children, she'd offer a class for the kids." Rubbing a hand across his forehead, Wyatt thought of all the planning for even one week of guests.

"The biggest challenge for us, not allowing interruptions to our regular businesses. Breeding, training, and selling horses."

"Plus boarding and teaching. You've always been good at working with new riders." Daisy picked up her fork, scooping up a bite of dessert. "This is so good. Would you like a bite?"

The joy on her face made him wish he could have more than a bite of pie. "Sure."

Sliding the fork under another bite, she held it toward him. Her gaze locked on his mouth as she slid the fork into it, wishing she could kiss him, taste the sweetness on his lips.

"You're right. It's great."

Pushing the plate between them, she lifted another bite to his lips. "I'm getting full. We should share the rest."

Instead of accepting the bite, he wrapped a hand around her wrist, his other hand sliding behind her neck. Drawing her toward him, he hovered over her luscious mouth for an instant before brushing his lips over hers.

He wanted to continue kissing her, lift Daisy onto his lap and wrap his arms around her. Inside a busy restaurant, surrounded by people one or the other of them knew, wasn't the best place to make out.

Leaning back, he dropped his hand from around her neck. "I've wanted to do that since we rode to Whistle Rock."

Settling back on her chair, her eyes lit with delight. "I'm glad you decided to kiss me now."

"Me too. Maybe we can do it again sometime."

A warm, infectious grin spread across her face. "Maybe we can."

Wyatt walked to the foreman's apartment at the back of the bunkhouse, hoping to find Virgil. Knocking, he was surprised when no one answered.

He'd driven Jasper and Virgil back to the ranch not long after lunch with Daisy. The doctor had given him an inhaler with corticosteroid, a prescription, instructions for avoiding triggers, and an action plan. Jasper grumbled about all of it.

Turning toward the barn, he spotted a group of men surrounding someone. "Gotta be Jasper," he murmured to himself, heading toward them.

As he walked, Wyatt couldn't help glancing around. What if they did add a dude ranch as a way to increase their profits and expand the ranch's name?

Each of the buildings had electricity and water. Extending those services to new cabins shouldn't be too difficult. If they started soon, they might be able to receive their first guests by late June.

Shoving both hands into sherpa-lined pockets, he shook his head at even considering opening a dude ranch by next summer. The better choice would be to spend his time expanding the horse breeding business. Between him and Jasper, they could double the income within a year.

"Hey, boss."

Wyatt glanced up to see Barrel waving, wanting him to join them. As he'd assumed, Jasper stood in the center of the group, no doubt regaling those around him with stories of his brief hospital stay. The fact they stood in freezing weather didn't seem to register on any of them.

"Jasper. Should you be out here?" Wyatt took a place next to the older man, noticing Virgil was nowhere in sight.

"You sound like my son."

"For good reason. The doctor said to take it easy for a few days. Virgil and I assured him you would." He glanced around the circle of men. "Don't you boys have work to do?"

"Sure do, boss." Barrel clasped Jasper on the shoulder. "Take care of yourself. We aren't ready for you to retire."

All the remaining men followed Barrel's lead before returning to their chores. When they were alone, Wyatt stepped in front of Jasper.

"You aren't expected to get back to work for a couple days."

Jasper's mouth twisted into a grimace. "I can't just sit around and do nothing."

"Understood. How about you supervise the men working in the barn? Virgil and I will deal with the work outside." When Jasper appeared to object, Wyatt continued. "Just for a couple days. Afterward, you decide what your body can handle until you're a hundred percent."

Grumbling, he nodded. "I can work with that. I'll go check out the work in the barn now."

Wyatt should've figured Jasper would start this afternoon. The man couldn't sit still.

"What'd you say to Dad?" Virgil glanced over his shoulder at his father, who was already yelling orders at the men.

"I reminded him of what the doctor said about rest. If he needs to get out of the apartment, he works in the barn for a few hours the next couple days."

"He'll complain no matter how much slack we cut him. What did you want to talk to me about?"

Wyatt started walking toward the bunkhouse. "Do you have coffee in the apartment?"

"It's easy to make."

"Good. I want privacy for this."

Virgil kept pace, opening the front door. "That bad, huh?"

The hint of a smile appeared. "That good."

Virgil set a mug of coffee in front of each of them a few minutes later, sitting across from Wyatt. "All right. You have your coffee. What's going on?"

"Pop wants me to take over management of the ranch."

Virgil almost choked on the swallow of coffee. "I sure as heck didn't see that happening so soon."

"Me either."

Cupping the mug with both hands, Virgil gave Wyatt a somber look. "It's because of his health."

"The doctor told him if he didn't slow down, he wouldn't be around much longer. He plans to take Mom on all the trips she missed out on over the years. Get this. Pop is looking at cruises."

Virgil barked out a laugh. "Your dad on a cruise? I'd pay to see that." Sobering, he took a sip of his coffee. "Running this place isn't going to be easy."

"How so?"

"The ranch hands will be fine. My guess is they'll do better under you than Anson. It's the suppliers who might give us trouble. They give your father trouble, and he's been working with them for years."

Stretching out his legs, Wyatt crossed them at the ankles. "What kind of trouble?"

"According to my father, they've worked on a handshake for generations. Anson goes in the first of each month and settles the account for the previous month. They're going to pressure you to use credit cards or more structured credit."

"So they can collect interest if I'm late paying," Wyatt speculated.

"Right. Brilliance Hardware was bought by True Value a few years ago. They'll push hard to get you on their system. I'd suggest you take Anson with you the first time. Or don't let on you're the one making the decisions." Virgil tapped fingers on the table. "Is anything changing on paper?"

"Doubt it. I'll just be picking up more responsibilities." Wyatt grinned. "Which means you'll be handling more too."

"How's that?"

"Jasper will continue as foreman. The asthma will change some of his duties. You'll need to pick up some of the work he's done for years."

Virgil nodded in understanding. "Haying, driving the horses and cattle to new pastures."

"Right. Anything which could impact his asthma."

"No problem, Wyatt. You don't need to worry about me taking on more work."

"There is one more thing where I'll need your help."

"What's that?"

"I want to expand our operations by offering dude ranch experiences."

Chapter Twelve

Daisy secured the last of the paintings to the wall, stepping back to admire the new arrangement. It had taken two days to get the shop back in shape, yet through it all, people showed up and pulled out their wallets.

Most were visitors passing through. One bought a large pastel she'd completed two months earlier of the Tetons from a rocky point on Whistle Rock Ranch. Virgil had guided her to the perfect spot, stayed until she'd taken forty pictures from different angles. In her heart, she knew the finished painting would be fantastic. It also paid her rent on the shop for two months.

"Good morning, Daisy."

She turned at the familiar voice, offering a warm smile.

"Hello, Braydon. I thought you'd still be up in Jackson Hole."

Brushing snow from his lambswool coat, he stepped farther inside. He'd become the financial planner to the rich and uber wealthy in the posh resort town north of Brilliance. Most clients weren't from Hollywood, San Francisco, or Seattle.

His preference was to work with well-heeled men and women from the Midwest or the South with second or third homes in Wyoming. Braydon believed them to be less maintenance than the prima donnas on the Pacific Ocean.

"Two clients didn't fly in because of the storm. They rescheduled for next week. The trip wasn't a waste, however. A realtor introduced me to a woman who sold her fitness clothing line for more zeroes than either of us will ever have. She's now a client."

"Congratulations, Bray. I know you'll do a great job for her."

Daisy found it hard to believe the Braydon of today was the same high school friend who took the bus or hitched rides with friends everywhere. To be fair, he always chipped in gas money, and was as far from being a bad guy as you could find.

Handsome, athletic, and brilliant with money, he just didn't spark her interest. Not the way Wyatt did. And truly, that was the only negative thing she could say about him. Except he kept asking her out. Instead of turning him down outright, she'd agree to coffee or lunch. Never dinner or a movie.

"What brings you in here today?"

"I heard you had some damage from the storm, and wanted to see if you needed help. It appears you've got it all taken care of. The shop looks as good as new, Daisy."

"Thank you." She flashed him a brilliant smile, knowing there had to be a great woman out there just meant for Braydon.

Lily had gone out with him a few times. As friends in high school, they could never make the transition to anything more. Daisy suspected it was due to her friend still being in love with Virgil Redstar.

"My mother is sick."

She whipped around to stare at him. "Will she be all right?"

Unable to meet her concerned gaze, he stared at the floor. "No. Cancer. Stage four."

She walked to him, grasping his arm. "Oh, my gosh, Bray. I'm so sorry."

"The doctor gave her two or three months."

"What about radiation or chemotherapy?"

The slow shake of his head told her everything. "The cancer is too far advanced."

Seeing him try to hide the moisture in his eyes, she wrapped her arms around him. "What can I do?"

Resting his chin on her head, he inhaled a shuttering breath. "There isn't much anyone can do."

"When did you find out?" Stepping away, she felt her heart squeeze for the handsome young man in such obvious pain.

"Yesterday. A neighbor found her at home. She'd collapsed and couldn't stand or get to a phone. The doctor said she first learned about it three months ago, but didn't want me to know. Mom thought she could beat it without worrying me." He turned away on a cough, which Daisy suspected hid a sob.

"When will they release her to go home?"

"I don't know. I'm meeting with the doctor again tomorrow. The truth is, I'm not sure she'll ever go home." The resignation in his voice broke her heart.

"I'm here for you, Braydon. Anything you need."

She remembered his father left within a year of his birth. His mother worked two jobs to pay for food and rent. She'd traded her alteration skills for new clothes for her son, buying clothes from thrift stores for herself. Everyone knew his frugal life and his mother's sacrifices were what drove him to succeed.

"I'll start a prayer tree for her. Would that be all right?"

Picking up his hat, he worried the brim. "I'd appreciate it, Daisy. I'm not up for getting the word out."

"I understand. This Saturday, you, Lily, and I will go to dinner."

"I'm not up for going out quite yet. Maybe after the impact of what's going to happen settles in. There's a lot to do, and not much time to get it done. Would you and Lily mind helping me with the final...you know...arrangements?"

"Of course. Anything you need, Bray. Just let me know."

The high school senior she'd hired to work after school arrived right on time. Daisy couldn't wait another minute to get out of the shop and to the ranch. It had been several days since she'd visited her horse. She needed the mindless work of grooming after the stress of the storm, cleaning up the shop, and the tragic news about Braydon's mother.

Tossing her handbag in the back seat of her GMC Acadia, she drove out of town toward Whistle Rock Ranch. Tension began to seep away within minutes, her tense muscles relaxing.

Turning toward Whistle Rock Ranch, the dusting of morning snow, bright sun, and clear skies reminded her of a holiday card. She thought it couldn't get better. Then it did.

A doe and two fawns dashed across the road no more than ten yards in front of her SUV. Slowing to a stop, she grabbed her camera, taking several quick shots before the three disappeared.

This was why she loved living in the area, the reason she'd come home after college. Not long before she'd left over four years earlier, her mother had married a retiree who spent summers in Brilliance. The rest of the year, he lived in a palatial home on the Florida coast.

Daisy's new stepfather had paid off the two-story home where she grew up. Her mother had kept the house open for when Daisy came back during vacations and the summer. She now lived in the three bedroom, three bath house several blocks from her Wind Song shop.

Continuing along the road, she turned into Whistle Rock Ranch, parking at the side opening of the barn.

Opening the back of the SUV, she slipped into her heavy jacket, boots, and gloves. As always, excitement flowed through her.

Daisy loved spending time with her mare. Whether it involved riding the trails, or just grooming, the companionship they shared provided a great deal of joy to the often lonely young woman.

"Hey, girl." Her voice triggered Honey to shake her head and walk toward her.

The corral by the barn wasn't large, holding three or four horses at a time. The ranch hands rotated the horses, allowing them a couple hours outside every day. Today, she planned to take Honey on a short ride on the road meandering through the ranch.

Clipping the lead line to the halter, she walked the mare into the barn, stopping near the tack wall. Honey's bridle, reins, blanket, and saddle were marked with Daisy's name.

"Thought I saw you enter the barn." Wyatt ambled toward her.

Shifting to glance toward him, her eyes widened when he lowered his head to brush a kiss over her mouth. Not satisfied with one, he clasped his hands on her shoulders, holding her steady for another, deeper kiss.

The sound of someone clearing their throat had Wyatt lifting his head. "I've been thinking about doing this all day," he whispered against her mouth. Stepping away, he turned to grin at Virgil.

Ignoring his friend's cocky expression, Virgil lifted Daisy's blanket and saddle, placing them on Honey's back. He could sense her embarrassment by the way she wouldn't meet his gaze.

"Good afternoon, Daisy."

"Um, hello, Virgil."

"Where are you riding today?" He slid her bridle from a hook, slipping it in place, letting her know kissing Wyatt shouldn't bother her.

"A short ride on the ranch road."

"Do you want company?"

Wyatt stepped beside her. "I'm going with her. Quinn's already saddled."

Virgil crossed his arms, quirking a brow. "Didn't you tell me you were riding out to check on the cattle?"

Wyatt checked the time, shrugging. "I'll ride out after we get back."

"It'll be too late."

"I'd love to ride out with you, Wyatt." Daisy walked Honey to the door. "Where's Quinn?"

"Right outside. We shouldn't be gone long, Virg. When we get back, the three of us should talk about the changes I talked about."

Daisy's brows drew together, but she stayed silent. There'd be time to learn what Wyatt meant when they returned. Mounting, she reined Honey outside to where Quinn stood.

Watching as Wyatt mounted, her mouth went dry. She couldn't think of another man who filled out a pair of

Wranglers as well as this cowboy. Staring at the way the denim stretched across his backside, she didn't notice Wyatt watching her, a smirk on his face.

"Are you ready?"

She startled at the amusement in his voice. "Just waiting for you."

"Then let's get going."

He led them around the buildings and corrals until they reached a gated pasture. Unlatching it, he waved her through before following and closing the gate.

"Where are the cattle?" Daisy's gaze swept over the horizon, seeing nothing except acres of snow.

"I'm hoping they're where we left hay for them yesterday. It's a larger herd, so they shouldn't be too hard to locate. Is this better than the road?"

"Absolutely. Although, the views from the road are hard to beat." She grinned at the doubtful expression on Wyatt's face. "You don't think so?"

Still recovering from the way her smile punched a hole in his chest, he stared at her. "What?"

Lips tight, she fought off a laugh. "The views from the road?"

"Uh, yeah. They're pretty good. Hold up a minute. I need to check something."

Dismounting, he walked around Quinn to where Daisy still sat in the saddle. Lifting his arms, he grabbed her around the waist, swinging her to the ground. Before she could question his actions, Wyatt wrapped his arms around her, capturing her mouth.

She hesitated a moment before gripping his shoulders. When his tongue glided over her lips, then delved inside, she moaned in pleasure. Moving her hands behind his neck, she tugged him down, not wanting to end what she knew would be over much too soon.

Chapter Thirteen

Wyatt knew they had to stop. Instead of lifting his head, his arms tightened around Daisy. He'd missed years of getting to know her while both were in college. Since seeing her when he'd first returned home, Wyatt had made up his mind to rekindle their long ago friendship.

A moan from deep in Daisy's throat reminded him there was a purpose to their ride. As pleasant as her lips felt against his, it was time to continue toward the cattle.

Lifting his head, he rested his forehead against hers, watching her eyes slowly open. His throat tightened at their unfocused, glazed appearance.

"We should ride on before the sun goes down." Rubbing his hands up and down her arms, the loss of her closeness punched him in the gut when she stepped away.

"You're right. This was a very nice reprieve, however." Going up on her toes, she pressed a kiss to his jaw. Swinging into the saddle, she watched as he did the same, still feeling her lips tingle. The sensation carried from the top of her head to the tips of her dark, red boots.

They rode in silence another ten minutes before Wyatt spotted the cattle. It didn't take long to check the remaining amount of hay and water in the large trough.

Counting the head, he sat back in the saddle, his shoulders relaxing.

"They're all here. The men will have to come out tomorrow to drop more hay and fill the trough." Checking the sky, his brows furrowed at the massive, dark clouds approaching from the south. "There should be plenty of time if we leave now."

Increasing their pace from the trip out, they rode nonstop until the barn came into sight. Slowing the horses to a walk, Wyatt reined closer to her.

"Stay for dinner."

"Thank you for the invitation." Daisy glanced over her shoulder. She didn't believe the black clouds would be as damaging as those of almost a week earlier, though they were moving straight toward them. "I should get back before the storm hits. Can I have a raincheck?"

"You're welcome here anytime." He stayed beside her as they entered the large barn where she boarded Honey.

Dismounting, he helped untack the mare, his gaze seldom straying from Daisy. He'd been trying to figure her out since returning from his aunt and uncle's ranch.

They'd had a good time on their few dates in high school. Her honesty and great sense of humor made her easy to be around. The same as him, she'd been born in Brilliance. At a year younger than him, they hadn't hung out together until his senior year.

Her best friend, Lily, had dated Virgil for two years during high school, which is how he met Daisy. After leaving for college, Wyatt never thought they'd connect again. Yet here they were, and this time, he was determined to see where their friendship could go.

Daisy worked in the backroom of the local photography studio. The owner, a good friend, had allowed her to use the high-tech application to complete the calendar of local ranching women. The file would be sent to the printer in a few hours, with a guaranteed delivery of one thousand calendars by November twenty-eighth.

Fifty businesses in town had committed to display and sell the calendars through December and January. After final negotiations with the Chamber of Commerce and City Council, it had been decided the profits would be split between two programs. Art scholarships would be provided for disadvantaged children to attend afterschool programs at Wind Song, with the rest going to the facility for abused families.

Reaching the last pages, she admired the picture of Margie with Wyatt on one side of her and Virgil on the other. They were both rugged, striking cowboys, although her attention locked on Wyatt.

After the kiss they'd shared, she found it hard to get him out of her mind. Nor could she satisfy her confusion as to his obvious desire. Where had it come from? He'd never shown such passion before leaving for college. What did his affections mean?

Probably nothing, she concluded. A few kisses meant nothing to a single rancher as sought after as Wyatt. He had to know about the large number of young women who waited impatiently for him to notice them.

She could think of four right off. All were daughters of successful ranchers or longtime town leaders. None held the dreams which motivated Daisy. Why should they? Any one of them would bring a great deal to a union with Wyatt. She even suspected at least two could come to love him, become a devoted partner and friend.

Daisy accepted she was a short-term diversion. Their friendship meant a great deal more to her than a few passionate kisses. Though she didn't see herself as less than the other women who sought his attentions, she was a realist.

Once Wyatt settled into his new role at the ranch, found time to reacquaint himself with the women his age, his interests would change. As for herself, Daisy had a business to run, and goals to achieve.

"Daisy, are you back there?"

"I'm at the computer, Lily. Come join me." Giving her closest friend a hug, she pulled up another chair.

Eyes wide, she leaned closer. "Is that the calendar?"

"It is. I'm almost finished."

"If the rest of the pages are as good as this one, the calendars will fly off the shelves. It's beautiful, Daisy."

Lily had helped her create the list and contact the ranching women shown on the pages. Her ideas appeared throughout the calendar, from the colors used to the quotes shown on each page. The two of them would deliver the finished product to the various businesses, and collect sales proceeds each Friday through January.

"I hope you're right. The printer will keep the price the same if we reorder after the first thousand."

"What quantity?"

"A minimum of three hundred." Daisy made a few changes to the last page, saved the document, and sat back. "I couldn't have done this without your help."

"Nonsense. Making ideas happen is in your blood. You could no more give up on something than quit expanding Wind Song. It has been your dream since high school. Do you still have your list?"

Daisy grabbed her messenger bag, her thumb and forefinger sliding out a single piece of paper. "I never travel without it."

Lily held out her hand. "Have you added anything to it?" Perusing the list, her eyes widened. "You haven't shown this to Wyatt, have you?"

"Never. You're the only person who's seen it. And don't you dare tell a soul."

"As if I would. I see the item is written in pencil. The others are in ink."

Taking the paper back, Daisy tucked it back into her bag. "I wrote it on a whim. We both know nothing will ever come of it. Well, I believe the calendar is ready to be sent off." She tapped a finger against her lips. "Maybe I should check it once more."

"How many times have you reviewed it?"

"Five."

"Let me do the sixth review. Fresh eyes and all that."

Standing, Daisy picked up her bottle of water before pacing to the front of the studio. "I'd appreciate your help."

"Take a walk. Or better yet, bring me back one of those fruit scones from the bakery. Oh, and a latte. I'll be finished when you return."

Crisp, cold air bathed her face when Daisy stepped outside. Inhaling a deep breath, she looked up and down the street. City workers had installed banners announcing a Thanksgiving lunch at a local church. Each included the caricature of a turkey holding a piece of pumpkin pie. They were the same banners the city hung up every year since her sophomore year.

Two weeks until the holiday and Daisy hadn't considered how she'd celebrate. Last year, she and Lily ate on campus. What would they do this year? Eat at the church? Or they could help prepare the meal and serve others. The idea appealed to her, and Lily would love it.

Reaching the bakery, she entered, stopping at the couple standing at the counter. Wyatt's hand rested on a woman's shoulder, her laughing expression fixed on him.

Unable to get her feet to take her back outside, she stared. Once the surprise wore off, Daisy realized she recognized the woman as the new veterinarian in town.

Tall, tan, with glorious red hair, Doctor Dorothea Zane possessed no flaws. Not a single one. Smart and kind, with a huge heart, she was the perfect match for Wyatt.

"Hello, Daisy. What can I get you?" The proprietor's voice had both Wyatt and Dorie turning toward the entrance.

"Daisy. I stopped by your shop, but you weren't there. The kid you hired wasn't sure where you were." Wyatt cocked his head, studying her face. "Are you all right?"

Shaking her head, she forced a smile. "Yes. Sorry. I've been staring at a computer for hours, finishing the calendar. Lily is reviewing it one last time while I grab scones and coffee. Did you see the banners for Thanksgiving?" She chastised herself at rambling.

Wyatt walked toward her, stopping a couple feet away. "What kind of scones? I'll buy them for you."

Waving a hand in the air, she stepped past him. "No need. Two blueberry and two peach, if you have them. Plus two lattes."

"It'll only be a few seconds."

"No worries." Knowing she was being a coward, she faced Wyatt. "I didn't know you were coming to town."

"I didn't know myself until an hour ago. Pop asked me to drive in to meet the new vet. You know Dorie, right?"

"Yes, we've met." Daisy stuck out her hand, giving Dorie's a friendly squeeze. "Good to see you. How is business at the clinic?"

"As you'd expect. Busy, which is great. I hate being bored."

"Here you are, Daisy." The middle-aged woman held out two sacks. One filled with scones, the lattes in the other. Paying, she headed to the door. "Good seeing you, Wyatt. Dorie. Have a good evening."

Careful not to slam the door, she headed toward the photography studio, unwarranted anger rushing through her. She didn't know why the idea of Wyatt with Dorie bothered her. Maybe because she'd been thinking it wouldn't be long before he met someone who truly caught his interest.

"Daisy, wait." Catching up to her, Wyatt took hold of her arm, spinning her around. "Where are you going in such a hurry?"

"I didn't want to interrupt you and the doc. We both know how busy you are."

Leaning down, he kissed her mouth, lingering a moment before lifting his head. "I'm never too busy for you."

Looking around him, she spotted Dorie watching them. "We have company."

"No doubt. You know how this town is. I have to stop at the drug store to pick up prescriptions for Pop and Jasper, then the feed store for a few items. Can I take you to dinner afterward?"

Daisy should say no, let him get back to the ranch, and her return to the shop. "I'd love to have dinner with you."

"Excellent. Think about where you want to go. Should I pick you up at the shop?"

"How about my house? Do you remember where it is?"

She shivered when he ran a hand down her arm. "Sure do. Is it still painted yellow with white trim?"

"I can't believe you remembered, and yes, it is."

"Great. See you about six." Kissing her cheek, he flashed a grin before heading back to the bakery.

Letting out a shaky breath, Daisy continued toward the studio, feeling a little foolish and a lot immature. Her behavior didn't seem to bother Wyatt as much as it humiliated her. She hoped Dorie didn't notice the rare rush of jealousy.

Daisy had never been the jealous type. Then again, the only man she'd ever cared about was Wyatt Bonner. Hadn't it been a couple hours ago when she'd convinced herself time with Wyatt would be short? After his kiss on the sidewalk, she may have to reconsider.

Chapter Fourteen

Wyatt parked across the street from Daisy's, the phone pressed to his ear. "I've already invited Daisy to dinner, Pop. I'm not going to cancel because you set me up with Dorie."

"You'll do this because it's what is best for the ranch and for you. That Raines girl isn't your future. The doc could be. Besides, I've already made a reservation for you at the Italian place, and I expect you to keep it."

Wyatt lowered the phone before saying something he'd regret. He respected his father, understood his need to put the ranch first. Most times, before his wife and family. Interfering in Wyatt's personal life couldn't happen.

"One time, Pop. I'll do this for you tonight, but if you interfere in my person life again, I'll head north to Bozeman. We both know Uncle Emmett would welcome me anytime."

A harsh chuckle came through the phone. "I've already talked to my brother. You aren't going anywhere, Wyatt."

Jaw tight, he worked to control the anger at his father's interfering ways. "What do you mean?"

"We agreed you aren't going north unless I've given my okay, and that's not going to happen. Of my three sons, you're the one who'll take over this ranch. I'm going to make certain your decisions are what's best for Whistle Rock."

"What I want doesn't matter?"

"Not unless it coincides with what I believe is important to keeping this ranch going."

Wyatt couldn't believe what his father was saying. As much as he loved the ranch, he'd leave if pushed too far. With his experience and degrees, Wyatt knew he wouldn't lack for offers. It would break his heart to venture out on his own, but buckling under his father's pressure would make him miserable.

"As I said, I'll take Dorie out tonight. Anything more will be my decision, not yours." Wyatt didn't wait for a response before ending the call.

Looking across the street, he hoped Daisy would be all right with canceling dinner. It wouldn't matter if he didn't like her so much. He hadn't expected to feel such a close connection with the cute blonde when he returned from Bozeman.

He'd enjoyed the times they'd gone out in high school, although he never saw them as long-term. She was too offbeat for his tastes. Daisy hadn't been raised on a ranch, knew nothing about raising cattle or horses.

Still, he'd never laughed as much with any woman as with her. Returning home, he hadn't planned to pick up where they'd left off. If it weren't for their ride to Whistle

Rock, he wouldn't have given a thought to dating her again.

She turned out to be more intriguing than Wyatt remembered. Within months of graduating, her shop had become a success. Over the years, she'd come up with the idea for the calendar, and was involved in several civic projects. He admired her drive, compassion, and positive outlook.

His stomach grew tight at what he'd agreed to with his father. One time, and he'd never do this to her again. Calling her number, she picked up on the first ring.

"Hey, Daisy."

"Wyatt. I saw your truck across the street. Are you going to come in or should I join you?"

Hesitating a moment, he let out a frustrated breath. "I've got to cancel. Pop has something he wants me to do. How about later this week?"

"Sure. Do what you have to."

"Thanks, Daisy. I'll call you later to reschedule."

"Yeah. See you, Wyatt." He felt horrible when she ended the call. All he could hope for was she didn't learn the reason he had to cancel was to take another woman out to dinner.

"I'm sorry Wyatt cancelled, Daisy. Still, this gave me the chance to take you out for your birthday. Did he know it was today?"

"No reason he would. He was in town doing errands and asked me to dinner. Thanks for doing this, Lily."

"Hey, we have to stick together. With your mom and stepdad in Florida, and my parents gone, we're each other's family. Right?" Lily held up her glass of iced tea, waiting until Daisy touched the edge with her glass of lemonade. Lily had lost her parents in a horrible two-car accident right before her college graduation ceremony.

Neither Daisy nor Lily were big drinkers, having wine once in a while, or a beer at barbecues. Tonight would've been a good occasion for the white wine they both enjoyed, but neither had been interested.

"Did you hear from your mom?"

Daisy shook her head, squelching another disappointment. Between Wyatt canceling and her mother forgetting her only child's birthday, it would've been a little depressing if it hadn't been for her best friend. Lily always remembered.

"Here you are. Lasagna for the birthday girl and gnocchi for you." The handsome waiter placed their plates down, his gaze lingering on Lily. Seeing her friend blush at his obvious interest, Daisy smiled. "Will there be anything else?"

"This will be fine. Thank you," Lily answered for both of them.

Scooping up a mouthful of lasagna, the fork stilled an inch from her mouth. Across the room, two people she recognized were being seated in a booth. Setting her fork down, a ball of pain lodged in her chest, the joy for her birthday meal evaporating.

"What's wrong, Daisy?" Lily glanced over her shoulder. "Isn't that Wyatt with the new vet?"

"Yes."

"Didn't he tell you he had to do something for his father?"

"Yes."

Lily's heart squeezed for her friend. "What a rotten thing to do. Do you want to have our meals packaged and we'll go back to my place?"

That's exactly what Daisy wanted to do, leave before Wyatt saw her. Unfortunately, she wasn't a runner. He'd made his choice, and now she had to make her own choice.

"No. It's my birthday, and I won't let Wyatt lying to me ruin it. Besides, I get free cake."

"Yes, you do." Lily could hear the pain in Daisy's voice, and wished she could do something about it. Other than walking to Wyatt's table and giving him a verbal thrashing, there wasn't much, except try to salvage what was left of Daisy's birthday dinner.

Able to get down only a few bites, Daisy gave up. The wonderful food tasted bitter in her mouth. Maybe it was best to leave. Watching Wyatt with his date would only make her more miserable.

Before she could get their waiter's attention, he appeared with three other employees. In his hand, he held a large piece of Italian wedding cake with a single candle. Then the four began to sing.

"Happy birthday to you, happy birthday to you, happy birthday, dear Daisy, happy birthday to you."

The song caught Wyatt's attention. Looking over, his gaze locked on Daisy. A pain he'd never felt before gripped his chest. When she spotted him staring, he couldn't breathe. The joy-filled woman he'd begun to care so deeply about looked as if someone had taken every ounce of happiness from her.

Not only had he cancelled their date to take another woman out, but it had happened on her birthday. It didn't matter that his father pushed him to do it, the final decision had been his. Wyatt failed as a friend, and as a man who didn't want to lose what they'd begun.

"Excuse me, Dorie." Standing, he'd planned to walk over and explain. Instead, he stopped when Daisy saw his intent. Holding up a hand, she shook her head, the meaning clear. There wasn't a chance she'd listen to him tonight.

Feeling every bit the lout he was, Wyatt sat back down.

"Isn't that Daisy?"

He nodded at Dorie's question. "Yes."

Leaning forward, she lowered her voice. "Why aren't you with her instead of me, Wyatt? It's obvious to anyone you have feelings for her. Did your father put you up to this?"

Embarrassment and an inkling of pride had him shaking his head. "I'm here because I want to be. Let's eat and enjoy our evening." Even as the words were spoken, Wyatt knew he'd already spoiled Daisy's night, as well as his own. He had no one to blame except himself.

Daisy ate what she could, determined not to let Wyatt see how much his deceit hurt. She'd been through worse in her life and survived. Tonight would serve as a lesson.

As much as she loved Wyatt, he would never be hers. Hot, heart-thumping kisses aside, he'd never fall for a woman without his father's approval.

Anson Bonner had made his feelings about Daisy clear more than once. She would never be good enough. If Margie Bonner hadn't taken such a liking to her, Daisy wouldn't be allowed on the ranch.

She didn't know why the man disliked her so much. All she'd ever been to him was kind and welcoming. Even when he'd been openly hostile, she'd held her tongue, smiled, and acted as if his antagonistic attitude didn't hurt.

Setting what was left of her meal in the refrigerator, she turned off the lights while heading to her bedroom.

Combing out her long, blonde hair, Daisy forced her mind on things other than Wyatt.

She and Lily had a calendar to print and distribute. They'd worked hard to convince twelve independent ranching women to participate, rearranging schedules to accommodate everyone. The proceeds would go a long way to helping disadvantage children and those from abusive homes.

Virgil's birthday was just a few days away. She assumed a party would be held on the ranch. Knowing she wouldn't be invited, Daisy already planned to invite him to dinner. His present had been completed several weeks earlier, and now sat on a shelf in her closet, wrapped and ready to go.

At dinner last night, she and Lily had discussed Thanksgiving. They'd agreed to help with the community meal at the church. Since neither had family close by, it would do both their souls good to share the day with others.

Setting down the brush, Daisy turned off her bedroom light and crawled under the covers. It had been a bittersweet day, one she hoped to never repeat.

Without Lily, it would've been a complete disaster. More sisters than friends, she knew they'd always be there for each other.

Closing her eyes, images of Wyatt played across her mind. The two of them at Whistle Rock, riding out to check on the cattle, racing the storm back to the ranch, him helping to secure her shop, and on the sidewalk where he'd kissed her for everyone to see. They were good images, the kind which made memories.

After tonight, Wyatt could only be a memory. He'd been a dream, a fantasy of the heart. The time had come to make new dreams. Attainable ones, where heartache wasn't allowed, and handsome cowboys didn't exist.

Chapter Fifteen

Wyatt couldn't sleep. He'd arrived home ready to have it out with his father, but the old man had already gone to bed. It was for the best. He didn't want to be the cause of another heart attack, and the conversation Wyatt envisioned could definitely trigger tension.

No matter his father's role in what happened, the decision had been Wyatt's. Instinct told him his father wouldn't kick him off the ranch. With his health a concern, Anson needed his oldest son to take over. Neither Jonah nor Gage had the desire to run the ranch.

Wyatt couldn't get Daisy's devastated look out of his mind. Until that moment, he hadn't accepted the depth of his feelings for her. He hadn't thought of love when spending time with her. Tonight, the emotion had slammed into him with the force of a two by four.

If only he could roll back the clock and tell his father to mind his own business. He had made it clear this would be the only time his father could interfere in his personal life. By the look on Daisy's face, the ultimatum might not matter.

Checking the time, he threw off the covers, and stalked across the room to his dresser. Grabbing his phone, he typed out a text to Daisy. An apology and request to meet so he could explain. Wyatt didn't know what he'd say, or if she'd listen. If the situation were reversed, would he be willing to hear her out?

Rereading the text, he pressed Send. He doubted she'd see it tonight. Probably be best if she didn't. Tomorrow morning would be soon enough, after she had time to consider what had happened. She had to know Wyatt would never hurt her on purpose. Even if not intentional, he had hurt her.

Setting the phone down, he walked to the window. Another storm was building. This time, from the north.

His mind went to the cattle. The horses had been brought into pastures close to the compound, where they could be tended to daily. The cattle were different. They'd been herded to pastures accessible by ranch trucks hauling trailers loaded with hay. Water trucks would follow, filling the large, round troughs.

Tomorrow, he'd send men out with hay and water. They'd also check for injured animals, strays, and predators that might be lurking about. Winter brought a slower pace, but not an end to the chores required around the ranch.

He'd also talk to Virgil about Jasper, as well as a few other issues. One of them being Lily. Wyatt had never spoken to his friend about the young woman he'd loved and left behind. He wondered if Jasper had pressured Virgil to end the relationship, the same way Wyatt's father was pressuring him.

Thinking about it now, his father had been glad Wyatt stopped seeing Daisy before leaving for Bozeman. As he recalled, they'd argued about it, somewhat the same as today. How had he forgotten his father's insistence he date someone more suitable? The determination in his father's voice back then mirrored his single-mindedness now. What did Anson Bonner have against Daisy Raines?

The question haunted him as he slid back under the covers and drifted off to sleep.

Wyatt did all he could to avoid his father the next two days. Not too different than how Daisy was avoiding him.

He'd yet to receive a reply to his text, or to the two others he'd sent since. Maybe it was for the best. There were problems at the ranch requiring his attention. Most were easy fixes, such as the split seam on one of the metal troughs, which had to be welded, or the sick cow the men had brought back to the barn for tending.

Not so simple were the two head of cattle found mutilated about two hundred yards from the herd. Virgil had ridden out to identify and track the predator. The search hadn't succeeded other than to confirm they had a wolf preying on their cattle.

Moving the herd wouldn't solve the problem. The wolf would continue tracking and killing, no matter where they drove the cattle.

Wyatt had already called the district game warden, who he expected within the hour. Until then, men were guarding the herd in three-hour shifts. The Bonner ranch had enough men to make this rotation work. Those with smaller spreads would find it difficult to rotate in less than six-hour shifts, exposing their men to below freezing temperatures for long periods of time. Even the constant campfires did little to cut down the chill after a few hours.

Tugging the ringing phone from his pocket, Wyatt's hope it was Daisy died at the sight of his father's image. Unable to ignore the call, he put the phone to his ear.

"Yeah."

"I heard about the dead cattle and wolf from Jasper. Why didn't you tell me?"

"Because you aren't running the ranch any longer, Pop. You're supposed to be resting and planning a vacation with Mom."

"That's not how this is supposed to work. I still want to be informed about everything."

"Then I'm the wrong man for this job. You want to fire me, fine. But I'm telling you right now, you aren't going to be told everything that goes on. It won't accomplish the reason you asked me to take over, and it'll only make me angrier at you than I already am. Why don't you go make a cup of hot chocolate and work on the books. I've gotta go, Pop."

A moment later, his phone rang again. This time, he ignored it. His mother was supposed to be making sure his father toed the line. So far, his father hadn't acknowledged the line, forget about following it.

Relaxing when the call went to voicemail, he continued his work in the barn, checking on every horse. Those in the largest barn were either boarded or needed special attention. Cordoned off at the back was a section for sick animals. Most could be tended to by Jasper or Virgil. A few required the vet's expertise. The last person he wanted to see right now was Doctor Dorie Worrel.

He'd been able to salvage their dinner after the disaster with Daisy. To her credit, Dorie was gracious, offering for him to take her home and head over to Daisy's. If he'd thought it would help, Wyatt would've taken her up on it. Unfortunately, that horse had ridden into the sunset when Daisy left the restaurant. If her lack of response to his texts meant what he thought, it could be weeks or months before she gave him the chance to explain in person.

Hearing a car outside the barn, he ran a hand down Honey's neck. "I'll be back in a bit, girl." Instead of the game warden he expected, Daisy climbed out of her SUV, dragging on a heavy coat before slamming the door. Wincing at the flash of irritation in her eyes, he found enough courage to walk toward her.

"Hey, Daisy. Any chance you came to see me?"

"None. I came to see Honey."

"She's doing great. I just left her stall." Wyatt didn't mention what he'd been doing. Daisy would find out soon enough.

"I'd rather check on her myself." Sweeping past him, she didn't look to see if he followed when she entered the barn. "There's my beautiful girl."

At Daisy's voice, Honey reared her head, shook it, and whinnied. Pawing at the ground, she whinnied again, anxious for Daisy to enter the stall.

"Wyatt was right. You look great. Has he been taking good care of you?" As the words fell from her lips, she noticed a small piece of paper tucked into Honey's halter.

Retrieving it, she read the note, then glanced around, confirming Wyatt hadn't followed her inside.

I'm sorry. Please let me explain.

Making a slow turn, she spotted another note tacked to the stall.

I miss talking to you.

Biting her lower lip, she spied one more piece of paper tied to the stall's latch.

Give me another chance, Daisy. I miss you.

A lone tear escaped, following a path down her cheek to her jaw. What was she to do? Maybe she should let him explain. If she didn't like his answer, they could still be friends, but go their separate ways.

"I know you're here somewhere, Wyatt Bonner. If you want to talk, come on out." When he didn't materialize, she closed the stall gate and began a half-hearted search.

Daisy was still hurt and angry at the perceived lie. He should've told her straight out he wanted to take Dorie to dinner. After the kisses he'd lavished on her, she'd believed their friendship was turning into more. Why hadn't he been honest?

Poking her head into the tack room, she saw no sign of him, though there was another note attached to Honey's bridle.

Dinner with Dorie wasn't what you think. Please let me explain.

"I'll let him explain, then decide what to do next," she mumbled to herself.

"That's all I can ask."

She whirled around to find Wyatt standing in the doorway. He looked so handsome in his dirty jeans, plaid shirt, scuffed boots, and hat set low on his forehead. No matter how incredible the view, he'd hurt her, trampled on the trust she'd given him. Daisy knew from experience how difficult it could be to regain someone's trust.

"Five minutes, then I'm going back to Honey's stall."

"I'll take whatever time you'll give me."

"The seconds are ticking, cowboy."

"I already told you Pop asked me to drive into town and visit with the new vet. What he failed to mention was he'd told her we'd be going to dinner together."

"When did you learn about dinner?"

"When I reached your house. I told him you and I had plans, and I wasn't going to change them."

"So he threatened you."

"How did you know?"

Dropping her arms to her sides, Daisy walked to Honey's saddle, running her hand over the leather.

"Because that's what your father does. If he doesn't get what he wants, he bullies people until they give in. Talk to anyone about his tactics. They aren't a secret."

"Did this start after I left for college?"

"Well before you left."

Wyatt knew his father had often used various degrees of bullying on him, his brothers, and even their mother. Threats of barring his sons from the ranch or cutting them out of his will weren't uncommon. Wyatt believed their father's tactics soured Jonah and Gage on the ranch. Both had picked majors giving them the option of leaving if their father didn't change. As for Wyatt, he had a standing invitation to return to his uncle's ranch.

"I thought Pop's threats were only directed at me and my brothers."

"Not at all. He's threatened Virgil more than once since he returned."

His jaw tightened as he absorbed her words. "Virgil would've told me."

"Would you have told him if Jasper threatened you?"

"It's not the same."

"Maybe not. The point is, you and Virgil have always protected each other, even if it got you into trouble with your father or his. It isn't a bad thing, Wyatt. All I'm saying is Anson has a temper and little patience. He also wants to win at any cost." She took a step closer. "Tell me the rest about Dorie."

"There isn't much, Daisy. You saw us at the restaurant. We ate and left, with no plans to see each other again."

"I don't know why not. She's a very beautiful woman, Wyatt. She's obviously smart, and from what others have told me, a good person. And don't forget, she comes from a wonderful family. Your father is friends with hers. I'm certain he sees it as a perfect match."

Wyatt watched as various emotions crossed her face. Conviction in her words, pain at what they meant, and resignation she wasn't as good for him as Dorie. He tossed them all aside, focusing on what he believed lived in her heart.

"I don't care about any of those. My decision won't be based on my father's desires. When I pick a woman to spend my life with, it'll be from here." He tapped a fisted hand to his chest.

Stepping to within inches of her, he rested his hands on her shoulders. "I want time to figure out what's going on between us, Daisy. Time to decide if we might have a future together."

Leaning down, he gave her time to step away. When she didn't, his mouth covered hers in a hungry kiss. Wrapping his arms around her, he continued to plunder her mouth, tasting coffee, peppermint, and the urgency of desire.

Continuing until they were both out of breath, he lifted his head without releasing his arms from around her. "The kiss was me telling you how much I like you and want a chance to see where this goes. Will you allow us another chance?"

Chapter Sixteen

Wyatt left the house early the next morning, successful in his attempt to avoid his father. Running into him before deciding his intentions and figuring out what to say would lead to disaster. Preparation would be critical for what he knew would be a serious confrontation.

He'd made plans to meet Daisy for coffee before visiting the bank, tack shop, and feed store. Wyatt had to learn for himself how his father operated.

Daisy had stayed another hour, talking with him while spending time with Honey. By the time she left, Wyatt believed they were back on solid ground, the problems his father created behind them.

Brilliance Coffee and Bakery was standing room only when he arrived at six-thirty. The townsfolk rose early, putting in long days, as had many of their ancestors. Just because they no longer raised cattle didn't mean their work ethic had changed.

Not seeing Daisy, Wyatt stood to the side while reading the overhead menu. There had to be fifty items listed, most available in regular and decaf. Hot brews, iced brews, and blended drinks flew out of the shop. All he wanted was black coffee and two of Lydia's outstanding cheese Danishes.

Lydia and his mother had grown up together, and married within a month of each other. Lydia's husband died in a one car crash on the I-90 eight years earlier. A stay-at-home mom her entire life, her only marketable skill was baking.

The Bank of Brilliance had turned down her loan request. The bank of Margie Bonner hadn't.

Few people knew Wyatt's mother provided funds for the shop, or that Lydia had paid off the loan within two years. While the two women celebrated the shop's success, they also plotted the opening of another location in Jackson Hole. It had been an instant success.

When the bell above the door chimed, Wyatt looked over to see Daisy walk inside. A broad smile appeared when she spotted him. Strolling right up to him, she leaned up to press a kiss to his lips. Instead of showing a hint of embarrassment, he kissed her back.

"Okay, you two, if you want to create heat, go into the kitchen." Lydia laughed as she said it, glad to see two of her favorite people together. "What can I get you?"

"A pumpkin mocha and a bear claw for me."

"And you, Wyatt?"

"Two cheese Danishes and a large black coffee." Pulling out a twenty and a ten, he set them on the counter.

"Let me get your change."

"No need, Lydia." Wyatt knew she always gave Margie and her sons discounts. They made up for it with generous tips.

"Find a table and I'll have it to you in a few minutes."

Instead of taking a table in the packed shop, they stood to the side. The two had already planned to eat at her shop so they could talk in private.

Daisy leaned close, lowering her voice. "Did you see your father this morning?"

"No. He was still in bed when I left."

Taking the bag of pastries from Lydia, Wyatt held the drinks as they covered the distance to her shop in a few minutes.

"I'll turn up the heat. Can we eat at the counter?"

"Fine with me." Setting the drinks down, he pulled out the pastries and napkins.

"I'm glad you didn't see your father this morning. It would've been too easy to say things you might later regret." Sipping her mocha, she watched him bite into the biggest Danish she'd ever seen Lydia serve.

Swallowing the bite with coffee, he looked at her. "You're right. After his heart attack, I don't want to do or say anything which might set off another one. I also can't let him run my life. I'm going to meet with some people this morning and get their input on him and how he does business. After what you said yesterday, I suspect my approach and his will be worlds apart."

"Do you have access to the ranch bank accounts yet?"

"No, and I hope to change that soon. Pop and Mom are talking about a month cruise starting after Christmas. I'll need access while they're gone. But what weighs on me is the way people fear him. Do you think my mother knows?" He knew his mother had been a huge supporter of Daisy and her shop. Perhaps they'd confided in each other.

"I don't know. She's tight-lipped about her family. Except..." Instead of finishing, she took a large bite of her bear claw.

"Except what, Daisy?"

Waving him off, she wished she'd said nothing.

"You can't start and not finish. Tell me what you were going to say." Reaching out, he ran a finger down her cheek, wanting to do the same with his lips.

"All right, but please don't say anything to her."

"Done."

"Margie hopes we get together."

Barking out a laugh, he leaned forward to press a brief kiss to her lips, tasting pumpkin and sugar. "No problem. We are together."

Grimacing, she again wished her mouth hadn't preceded her brain.

"There's more, isn't there?"

"Can we forget I said anything?"

"Spill it, Daiz."

A small grin curved her lips at the use of the nickname he'd given her in high school. "Margie hopes we end up together. You know. Marry, have kids." Burying her face with both hands, she groaned. "Geez, this is so embarrassing."

Jaw dropping, he stood before her wide-eyed. "My mother said she hopes we marry?"

"Yes...no...well...yes. She said almost those exact words. Don't worry, Wyatt. I know what we have is unlikely to end in marriage. You can relax."

Something about the tone in her voice bothered him. Perhaps the embarrassment of repeating his mother's words. Or resignation she already knew a future with him would never happen. Maybe it was something else.

"Daisy?"

Shaking her head, she started to walk to the backroom. As she turned away, a large, warm hand gripped her arm, holding her in place.

"Don't walk away. Would a life with me be so bad?"

Brows knitting together, she gaped at him. "Of course not. I don't know how a life with you would be, Wyatt. It's much too soon to make any decisions. First, we'd have to fall in love. Even then, it might never come to marriage. There are too many unknowns."

"By unknowns, do you mean my father?"

Shrugging, she began picking up the leftover pastries. "I'm certain he'd have something to say about it. You know what, let's just drop this. I told you what Margie said. Beyond her hopes, we have our own dreams. I don't even know what yours are. Do you?"

It was a fair question. There was so much he wanted to do with the ranch. So much he believed he could accomplish with the help of Virgil and his brothers. A grin broke through the confusion.

"I want to grow the ranch into the largest and most respected Paint breeding program in the U.S. I also want to open the ranch to those who've never experienced anything except living in a city."

"A dude ranch."

"Of sorts. A dude ranch, outdoor adventure camp, and lifestyle experience unlike what can be found anywhere else. A one stop western adventure that brings families back year after year."

"Wow. When you dream, you do it in a big way."

"Too much?'"

Happy to be off the topic of their future, she shook her head vigorously. "Not at all. What you want to do is exciting and challenging. I've always believed you could do anything you set your mind to. To you, obstacles are temporary challenges meant to be overcome."

The compliment humbled him. "What is your dream, Daisy?"

Chuckling, she glanced around her shop. "Expand Wind Song. Bring in more artists. Offer more classes. Most importantly, make art fun so more people will explore it."

Studying her in a new way, he pulled her against his chest. "Getting to know each other while exploring our dreams could be a lot of fun."

And it could lead to heartache, she thought, but refused to voice it. "Yes, a great deal of fun."

Leaving the bank a few hours later, Wyatt wondered why he thought pursuing a dream no one understood could be fun. The bank manager grasped the dude ranch concept. The western adventure idea took him a little longer. When the assistant manager joined them, she found the proposal exciting. She believed it would set Whistle Rock Ranch apart from other dude ranches.

Once he understood, the manager requested a business plan with financial projections. He also made it clear Anson's approval would be required to move forward. The banker didn't want to put too much time into considering a loan if Anson vetoed the project. Wyatt conceded it was a real possibility.

Walking back to his truck, he decided the best way to obtain his father's backing would be to get his mother behind the concept. He believed getting her excited about the western model would be easy.

When Jonah and Gage came home for Christmas, Wyatt would sit down with them. He knew both would go for the idea. They'd need Jonah's help preparing financial projections, and he expected Gage to jump at the chance to design the outdoor adventure concept.

Wyatt's meetings at the feed store and tack shop confirmed what Daisy had told him. The owners of the two companies were careful about what they revealed. Without implying Anson threatened to pull his business if they didn't give him larger discounts, each made it clear if Wyatt bargained the same as Anson, the ranch might be better off ordering from dealers outside of Brilliance.

Assuring them he wasn't his father, Wyatt shook hands with each one. They'd been as candid as they dared. No matter how difficult the customers, when living in a smaller community, you couldn't afford to burn bridges with anyone.

Unlocking the truck, he sent a quick glance at Daisy's shop. If there wasn't work at the ranch waiting for him, he'd try talking her into lunch.

Climbing into the driver's seat, Wyatt wrapped his hands around the steering wheel while thinking of their conversation earlier. According to Daisy, his mother would have no problem if they fell in love and decided to marry. Odd, since they'd been seeing each other such a short period of time.

Wyatt liked Daisy a lot, enjoying every minute they spent together. He planned to see her a great deal more over the next year. It didn't mean he loved her or planned marriage. They were a long way from considering a life together.

Even as he had the thought, Wyatt pictured Daisy living on the ranch, rounding up a passel of kids with her beautiful hair and smile, and his eyes. Realizing where his thoughts were heading, he shoved the image from his mind.

Marriage? Children? Not a chance.

Shaking his head, he pulled out into traffic, chuckling at the ridiculous idea.

Chapter Seventeen

"This is a great space, Daisy. Plenty of room, and the food is wonderful." Lily watched guests crowd into the room used for special gatherings at Dulcy's Grill and Tavern.

"I asked Chip Draper if he knew of a place." Daisy chuckled, remembering the surprise on his face. "He said to follow him. When he opened the double doors, I knew this was the perfect place. Virgil loves their food, and no one is expected to dress up." She nodded toward Jeramy Barrel and another ranch hand. "Since most work on ranches, it seemed right."

"Well, it is." Lily glanced over her shoulder at the door. "When do you expect Virgil and Wyatt?"

"I asked Wyatt not to get here until seven, which should give everyone plenty of time to get here." Finishing the last of the centerpieces, Daisy faced her best friend. "I'm so glad you decided to come tonight. Even after eight years, I know it's hard to be around him."

"It is hard, and probably always will be. I need to move on."

Daisy stared at her a moment, a grin lifting the corners of her mouth. "Is there someone special you haven't told me about?"

"No, nothing like that."

"With all the doctors you work with, I would've thought one would catch your interest."

Eyes dancing with merriment, Lily shook her head. "It's a small hospital. The staff count is low, and most of the docs are married, engaged, or seeing someone."

Daisy waved at a group of people who went to school with Virgil. "All those could change."

Lily lifted a glass of water to her lips, taking a long swallow. "Honestly, not one makes my heart tick faster. How do you feel when you see Wyatt?"

Caught by surprise, she blinked a few times. "We aren't talking about me."

"Come on. Tell me your stomach doesn't flutter and your heart doesn't race when he walks into a room. And be honest."

"All right. Both of those do happen."

"That's what I want."

"Do you still feel that way when you see Virgil?"

Lily smiled at one of the men from Whistle Rock Ranch, wishing she'd feel something for another man. Eight years, and she still loved Virgil.

"Quiet everyone. They just walked into the restaurant." Barrel stood by the door, peeking through the crack. "All right. Get ready." Taking a step backward, he gripped the doorframe.

Wyatt set a hand on his friend's shoulder. "Go on inside, Virgil, so we can start the celebration."

Virgil raised a hand in greeting, taking a couple steps into the room. "Did you set this up?"

"Ninety percent of it was Daisy and Lily."

Whirling around, one brow lifted in disbelief. "Lily?"

"Yep. She offered to help."

Virgil didn't have a chance to ask more questions before friends surrounded him.

"Go on and wish him a happy birthday, Lily."

"I don't know. He's got all his buddies around him. Maybe I should just go."

"Don't you even consider walking out now. He's seen you, and will expect you to say something. Come on. I'll go with you."

Placing a hand on Lily's back, Daisy gently propelled her toward where Virgil stood engulfed by his friends. Several feet before reaching him, Lily dug in her heels, refusing to go another step.

"I can't. You go, Daisy, while I check on the food."

"All you have to do is say hello. Go on now while I check on the food with Chip."

The decision was taken from her when Virgil broke from the crowd. Without taking his gaze from her or breaking his stride, he crossed the room to stand within a foot of her. It was the closest they'd been to each other in eight years.

They were so close, she could feel his warm breath, inhale the unique scent which had her heart racing. Standing erect with his long, black hair combed into a ponytail, his caramel-brown eyes bore into her.

"Wyatt told me you helped Daisy put this party together."

The deep timbre of his voice washed through her, as it always had, drawing her to him. Today, she stood her ground, showing no reaction to being so close she could press her hand to his chest.

"I didn't do much. Happy birthday, by the way."

"Thank you, Lily."

"You're welcome. I'll let you get back to your friends." Beginning her retreat, she stopped when his hand reached out to touch hers.

"Please, don't go. Maybe we could talk for a bit?"

A familiar pain shot through her, one she wasn't prepared to deal with tonight. "I thought I could do this, talk to you as if nothing had ever happened between us. I mean, after all this time, I thought it would be easy." Taking a step back, she forced herself not to look away. "It's not."

"You're braver than I am, Lily."

Choking out a laugh, she shook her head. "I'm not brave at all."

"Yes, you are. I've wanted to talk to you for eight years, but never found the courage. I'm the one who messed everything up between us. You don't know how many times I've wanted to take back what I said that day."

Holding up her hand, she rocked on her heels, wanting to get away. "Please, Virgil, don't say anything more."

"Hey, birthday boy." Barrel lifted a chin at Lily while holding out a beer toward Virgil. "It's time to lighten up and enjoy your party."

"He's right. Happy birthday, Virgil. I hope you have a wonderful evening." Before he could stop her, Lily turned, leaving the room and the party behind.

Wyatt and Virgil rode home in silence after the party. The large box in the seat behind them was filled with gifts. Most were funny tokens of friendship, a few more expensive and personal. His favorite present came from Wyatt.

"Thanks again for the painting. It's the best present anyone's ever given me."

"Better than the Superman cape?"

Virgil threw back his head on a laugh. "That was pretty special. But I was eight. Everything was special."

"My guess is you still have it under your pillow."

"You got me there. Just don't tell my father. He'll kick me out of the apartment."

Chuckling, Wyatt turned off the highway onto the ranch road, which ran through part of the Bonner property. "You and Jasper are coming to the house for Thanksgiving, right?"

"Wouldn't miss it. Nacho starts cooking three days in advance. Other than Christmas, it's the best meal of the entire year. Will Daisy be there?"

"I haven't asked her yet."

"Why not?"

Pulling into a spot next to the barn, Wyatt turned off the engine, not making a move to get out. "Daisy will want to bring Lily."

"I know."

"And you don't mind?"

"Not at all. She came up to me tonight. We didn't talk long..." Virgil shrugged. He stared through the windshield at a clear sky covered with stars.

"I'll be darn. After eight years, it's about time the two of you spoke. Does she have any idea how you feel about her?"

"The restaurant wasn't the best place to talk about my failings."

"Maybe you can get her alone on Thanksgiving. Work on reviving your friendship."

"I'm not going to push her, Wyatt. For now, I'll take what I can get." Opening his door, Virgil climbed out. "Did you hear that?"

"What?" Wyatt walked to the front of the truck, carrying the box of gifts.

"Sounded like a dog."

Holding the box out to Virgil, he listened, hearing nothing. "Probably a coyote."

The sound came again, both men turning toward it.

"A dog," they both said at the same time.

"Out there." Virgil pointed to the far side of the barn. Setting the box down, he jogged around the building, Wyatt right behind him.

When the whining noise came again, they continued toward one of the new storage sheds. Slowing as they got close, Virgil walked around one side while Wyatt took the other. Reaching the back at the same time, both stopped at the sight of an emaciated female dog covered in blood. Her coat was so crusted it wasn't possible to determine her color.

"I'll grab blankets out of the barn while you check her injuries." Wyatt took off at a jog.

Approaching slowly, Virgil spoke in a soothing voice, his gaze roaming over the injured dog. "Hey, girl. I won't hurt you." Dropping to his knees, he ignored the urge to reach out and stroke her coat. When taking classes for his pre-veterinary degree, there'd been a speaker who lost a hand to an injured dog.

Inching closer, Virgil continued speaking as he searched for wounds. He sucked in a breath when he spotted tooth marks in at least two places. Whatever attacked her had been going for a kill.

"Here you are." Wyatt held out two blankets, a bucket filled with water, and several clean cloths. "Have you figured out what happened?"

"There are two places where she's been bitten. I'm guessing a larger animal. Some type of predator. I need to get antibiotics into her before the wounds become infected. First, let me see if she'll let us clean her up. It'll take both of us."

"Tell me what to do."

Their first attempts were thwarted when she growled, snapping at them when either got close. The ranch kept sedatives for horses and cattle, but nothing for a smaller animal. They'd been prescribed by the previous vet, who'd sold his practice to Dorie, and now spent half the year in Arizona.

"I don't know how to cut the dose for a dog."

Wyatt continued his attempts to get closer, each time withdrawing when she growled. "You may not have to. She's tiring, Virgil. It won't be long before she's too weak to resist."

"There's something else I want to try." Virgil cleared his throat and began singing. It was a simple song, one his father would sing when his young son couldn't sleep.

Several minutes passed before his low, soothing voice began working on the injured dog. Her eyelids grew heavy as she fought to keep them open. When her attempts to stay awake failed, her body relaxed as she fell into a deep sleep.

"Let's get her into the barn. It's too dark to see much, and I want a good look at her wounds."

Spreading out a blanket, they lifted the dog on top, relieved when she didn't wake up. Just as they bent down, a shout came from behind them.

"What do you have?" Barrel hurried toward them, sucking in air when he stopped. "What happened?"

Virgil explained, ending with their plan to carry her to the barn.

"Let me carry her." Not waiting for a response, Barrel slipped his arms under the injured dog, easily holding her against his chest.

Grabbing the additional blanket, bucket, and rags, Virgil and Wyatt followed.

Wyatt glanced around as they reached the barn, wondering if whatever attacked the dog was stalking them. "Could it have been a wolf?"

Virgil watched as Barrel set the injured animal on a table. "That would be my guess. What I don't understand is why the predator left while the dog was still alive."

"Maybe another animal ran it off."

"Or someone came upon them and scared the other animal away." Virgil took a long look at the dog. "Barrel, call Doc Worrel."

Wyatt stood next to Virgil, getting a good look at the wounds. "Are you certain we need to get her out here? I'd prefer you work on the dog."

Spreading the fur away from one of the wounds, Virgil studied the size of the laceration. "It's not a good idea for me to treat animal bites that fully penetrate the skin. While Barrell calls her, I'll shave the fur and clean the wounds with warm water, then dry them. I don't want to do more until Dorie has had a chance to check her over."

"Should I call her or not?" Barrel asked.

"Call her. Tell the doc what you know. Maybe she can walk Virgil through helping the dog over the phone."

"I'm on it." Rushing out of the barn, they could hear Barrel's voice before he returned to the table. "The doc's coming out. She has antibiotics for bite wounds. Says to go ahead and shave the area and clean with warm water. I told her you were already on it."

A low, pitiful whining drew their attention back to the dog. Wyatt ran a hand over the animal's head, whispering close to her ear while Barrel helped Virgil shave the fur away and clean the lacerations.

"I understand there's an injured dog in here." Dorie walked in, her pink and black vet bag in one hand. Setting it on the table, her attention focused on the dog.

"Good job cleaning the wounds. They are definitely bite marks." Opening the bag, she tugged on Nitrile gloves before setting out antiseptic ointment, lidocaine, a suture kit, hydrogen peroxide, gauze pads, penicillin, and tweezers.

Working with experienced hands, she removed tiny bits of rock and sand before sanitizing with hydrogen peroxide, and suturing the wounds.

"Do you want to take her back to the clinic or do you prefer keeping her here?"

Wyatt looked at Virgil, who answered. "Here."

"I'll leave what you'll need. My guess is she'll be up and running around in less than two weeks. What's her name?"

Stroking the dog's fur, a smile appeared on Wyatt's face. "Trooper."

"Great name. With you three keeping watch on her, Trooper's a lucky dog. I'll be back in a few days to check on her. Call if you need me sooner."

Chapter Eighteen

Daisy dusted the last of the bookshelves in the living room, then moved to the antique buffet. Her mother had positioned the ornate piece against the wall between the living and dining rooms not long after Daisy's birth. Months before her father walked out on both of them.

Straightening, she took a slow turn around the room, making certain nothing had been missed. The living room always ended her Sunday ritual of cleaning the older clapboard house. She felt a good deal of pride in what her mother accomplished after her husband left. Working no less than two jobs, she'd made enough to keep the house through some very bad times. Remarrying after years as a single parent, her mother lived in Florida with a wonderful man who adored her.

Checking the clock on the fireplace mantel, Daisy rushed to put the cleaning supplies away. Wyatt would be arriving in an hour for an early dinner after her invitation at church that morning.

He'd somehow found enough room in the pew to sit next to her, their thighs and knees touching from the close quarters. Daisy recalled how she'd grown warm, then hot at being plastered against him. Even though they'd kissed more than once, his closeness affected her more each time. When the service ended, she'd walked out beside him, his fingers threaded through hers.

Before thinking it through, she'd invited him to dinner, then scrambled to come up with something to cook. Driving straight to the grocery, she found a discounted package of large filet mignon steaks. A bag of fresh green beans, mushrooms, bacon, and sweet onions were added to the meat, along with red skin potatoes. Placing the ingredients for peach cobbler in the cart, relief had washed over her.

Glancing around the kitchen, her gaze swept over the roasted potatoes, green beans, and cobbler. She'd warm them while cooking the filets. Being honest, she hoped Wyatt would volunteer to cook them on the grill under the covered porch.

Hurrying upstairs, her steps slowed. Her mind went back eight years to the afternoon Wyatt had told her he'd be leaving for Montana. He'd been excited for the change, ready to attend Montana State, and learn about his uncle's dude ranch.

Not once had he mentioned missing her, or staying in contact. In return, she'd kept her feelings for him hidden. He'd never known she'd thought about him often, and missed him terribly during those eight years.

Slipping into a pink sweater with embroidered teapots of various colors, she took a few minutes to braid her hair. Memories of him leaving all those years ago swamped her.

Their talk of a few days earlier came to mind. Neither knew if their future would include the other. The idea of him falling in love with someone else and marrying caused her chest to squeeze. She so wanted her future to include Wyatt.

Daisy allowed herself a few minutes to consider how deep her feelings were for the handsome rancher. Most would consider her a dreamer, with fairy dust for brains, a person whose mind was often filled with fantastical notions. She'd found their assumptions interesting, but never denied them.

Her fanciful dreams had gotten her through high school, then college. Without her goal of opening Wind Song, she wouldn't have made it through all the tedious classes and endless homework. She wondered if those same classes bored Wyatt. Probably not. He enjoyed all kinds of learning, whether or not the subject had an impact on his plans.

Was a future with Wyatt one of her fanciful notions? Would their time together end with her brokenhearted, watching as he found love with someone else? As much as Margie wanted them together, Anson wanted the exact opposite. Would Wyatt cave under his father's pressure, and walk away from Daisy, the way her father had left years earlier?

Was her time with Wyatt a certain path to certain heartache?

Hearing the doorbell, she checked the mirror, forcing a smile before rushing down the stairs. Without checking the peephole, she drew the door open, and froze.

A middle-aged man of above average height stood on the porch. He stared at her, not making a move to introduce himself.

"May I help you?"

Clearing his throat, the man shifted from one foot to another. "You're Daisy..."

It wasn't a question, which confused her. "Yes. I'm Daisy Raines. And you are?"

"You don't remember me, do you?"

Brows drawing together, she studied his face. His green eyes and thinning blond hair were in contrast to a ruddy complexion. They were also familiar. A knot of dread grew in her stomach as she realized who he was.

"You're Warren Raines. My father."

"Yes."

Feeling her body shake, she gripped the door handle, vaguely hearing the slamming of a car door. Tearing her gaze away, she looked past him to the street. Wyatt strolled toward the house. He must have seen the shock on her face because his pace increased. Bounding up the steps, he moved past the older man to stand beside her. Resting his arm over her shoulders, he looked between the two.

"Daisy?"

Reaching out, she took his free hand in hers. "Wyatt, this is my father, Warren Raines. Warren, this is my good friend, Wyatt Bonner."

Wyatt's hand tightened on hers at the knowledge the man on the porch was her father. The same man who'd left his family behind years earlier.

Nodding at the older man, he made no move to extend his hand. "Mr. Raines."

"You must be one of Anson Bonner's sons."

"The oldest. What brings you to Brilliance?"

Warren looked at Daisy. "I wanted to see my daughter."

A chilling silence engulfed them. Daisy didn't know what to do, except offer basic hospitality.

"Would you like to come inside for a few minutes?"

Warren sent a look at Wyatt before answering. "I'd appreciate it. I promise not to stay long."

Settling a hand on the small of Daisy's back, Wyatt walked inside behind her. He felt no guilt at leaving Warren to take up the rear. Thick disdain for the man who'd sired Daisy gripped his heart, making it hard to consider giving him even the slightest break. Wyatt couldn't imagine what it would take for a man to leave his wife and baby daughter behind, with no care for their future well-being.

"It's lovely, Daisy."

"Thank you. Would you care for something to drink, Father?"

"Coffee, if you have it."

"Wyatt? I have the root beer you like."

A warm smile spread across his face, relieving the tension at having her father arrive unannounced. "That's what I'll have."

Watching as she walked the short distance to the kitchen, Wyatt motioned for Warren to sit down, then chose a chair across from him. Lowering his voice, he pinned the older man with a calculating glare.

"Why are you really here, Mr. Raines? Please don't tell me it's about seeing a daughter you abandoned twenty-six years ago."

Warren set his hat down beside him, clasping his hands together. "There is no other reason."

"I doubt that. Do you need money?"

Chuckling, the older man glanced away. "A man can always use extra cash, although I have missed my daughter."

Disappointed, though not surprised, Wyatt appreciated the man's honesty. "How long do you plan to stay in Brilliance?"

"Not long. There's a job waiting for me in Sheridan."

"What kind of job?"

"I'm a mechanic. There's not much I can't fix."

"Sorry. It took a little longer as the coffee machine was turned off." Daisy handed a cup of coffee to her father before giving Wyatt a glass filled with ice and a can of Barq's root beer. "Not knowing what you take, I brought sugar and cream." She set it down next to the cup of coffee.

"Black is fine." Taking a sip, Warren held it on his lap. "It's good."

"My stepfather bought one of those single serve coffeemakers since he prefers his darker than Mom's."

"So it's true."

Sitting down close to Wyatt, her gaze narrowed on Warren. "So what is true?"

"Your mother remarried."

"Yes, and she's incredibly happy." Drinking from her glass of water, Daisy tried and failed to feel anything for her father. She didn't hate him, nor did she love him as a daughter normally would. Caring about his welfare was the closest she could come to defining her feelings.

"I understand you have a store in town."

She relaxed, glad for the change in subject. "Yes. Wind Song is my art store."

"I walked by it earlier. A little pricey for me, but I must say the items are beautiful." Warren continued to hold his cup, as if setting it down would signal the end of his visit.

"All the pieces are unique. One of a kind, so they are a little more expensive than similar items that are mass-produced." Standing, Daisy walked to the bookshelf. Reaching for a small frame, she held it in front of her for a moment. Before changing her mind, she walked back to her father.

"I'd like you to have this."

Warren's hand shook a little as he took the small painting from her hand. Studying it, a tear escaped, slipping down his cheek before he could stop it.

"It's a painting of me at my college graduation. I know it's not much—"

Warren held up a hand, stopping whatever else she meant to say. "This is the nicest present anyone has ever given me. I'll keep it with me. Always."

"Everything is excellent, Daisy. I didn't know you could cook." Wyatt placed another forkful of green beans in his mouth, a grin forming as he chewed.

"Lily and I had an apartment while in college. Eating out was too expensive. We took turns cooking." Her father's visit still weighed on her.

He'd left soon after receiving the painting. Before climbing into his truck, she noticed Wyatt handing Warren something, which appeared to be money.

"What did you hand my father before he left?"

Wyatt didn't consider lying. "A hundred dollars."

Setting down her fork, she cocked her head to one side. "For what?"

"He's starting a job in Sheridan, but was short on gas money. I wanted to make certain he reached his destination."

"I'll pay you back."

"No, you won't. It was my choice to give him the money. How are you doing after his visit?"

"All right. He wasn't what I expected."

Slicing a piece of steak, he held it above the plate. "In what way?"

"I wanted to dislike him. Instead, I felt little. It would be fine if I saw him again. I'd also be fine if we never cross paths again. What does that make me?"

Picking up his glass, he swallowed down the steak with root beer. "A normal daughter whose father abandoned her. It's been twenty-six years. Do you even remember him?"

"Only from pictures."

Reaching out, he wrapped a warm hand around her wrist. Letting his thumb rub circles over the soft skin at her pulse point, his voice gentled.

"It's not your fault you feel little for him. You once mentioned never hearing from him in all the years he was gone. No birthday cards or Christmas gifts. No phone calls or visits. Don't berate yourself for not loving him in the same way as most daughters love their fathers. No one would expect you to."

"Maybe *I* expect me to."

"Then that's something you'll need to figure out on your own. Know I'll be here if you want to talk." When she didn't respond, he pushed back his chair and stood. "Did you say there's a peach cobbler?"

"And ice cream."

"Excellent. We'll each have some, then take a walk.
Sound good?"

"Sounds wonderful."

Chapter Nineteen

"Do you remember Braydon Stiles from high school?" Daisy's hand rested comfortably in his, the warmth seeping through her.

The temperature had dropped by over ten degrees since they'd begun their walk after dessert. Wyatt had raved about the cobbler, the topic of her father forgotten as they covered several blocks. Daisy couldn't recall the last time she'd been so happy.

"Braydon? Was he in my class or yours?"

"My class. He wasn't too involved in activities, as they had little money. Bray is now a financial planner with an impressive client base."

"Yes, I do know who he is. Mother told me she's using him for her funds. She's very impressed. Why?"

"His mother is dying."

Wyatt stopped, turning to face her. "Dying? He's certain there's no hope?"

"She has stage four cancer. Radiation and chemotherapy are no longer an option."

Continuing along the sidewalk, he led her into a small café, taking seats inside. After she ordered tea and him coffee, he grasped her hand again.

"How is Braydon taking it?"

"Not well. His mother is all he has. I'm concerned about him."

"He's not married?"

She shook her head. "No fiancée or girlfriend, either. I do meet him for coffee or lunch sometimes. He's smart and very nice. I think he lacks confidence when it comes to women."

"Then he's not much different from any other man."

Laughing, she placed her other hand on top of their joined ones. "You're the most confident man I know."

"If it involves the ranch. Women are another matter." Hearing his name, Wyatt retrieved their drinks, placing the tea in front of her. "Are you planning to do anything to help Braydon?"

"Lily and I are working together to come up with a plan for after his mother passes. We've also notified the church women of the situation. They're setting up a meal schedule for him. I'll be preparing Thursday dinners and Lily will prepare them for Mondays. We plan to eat with him on those days unless he prefers to be alone. I just feel so bad for him."

"Let me know what I can do. I'll make sure Mom knows what's going on."

Adding cream, she stirred, thinking about what he'd said about confidence around women. "Did you date many women while in Montana?"

"A few. With school, the rodeo team, and work on the ranch, there wasn't much time."

Sipping her tea, she watched him over the rim. "Anyone special?"

Glancing away, he didn't respond for several seconds, indicating to Daisy there had been someone. "Sort of."

"What does 'sort of' mean?"

Holding his cup, he sat back. "I met someone my sophomore year. She was on the rodeo team. There was something about her that caught my interest and held."

Stomach clenching, she fought the growing unease. "For how long?"

"Two years."

That was much longer than she and Wyatt had been together. "Why aren't you still with her?"

Resting his arms on the table, he stared into what was left of his coffee. "No one knows about this except Virgil."

Which told her the relationship was very important to him. "You don't need to say more, Wyatt." Pouring more cream into her already off-white tea, she wondered if the woman was still important to him.

"I don't know if I loved her or not. Robyn was two years older. She went on to graduate school while I was in my junior year. She received her MBA at the end of the year and took a job in Bozeman. It wasn't her ideal position, but she decided to stay to be close to me."

Voice flat, she forced a small smile. "She loved you, and you loved her."

Lips pressed together, he watched as several people entered the café. Turning his attention back to her, he didn't respond to her comment.

"Robyn wanted to get married."

Jaw dropping, she clamped her mouth shut. Feeling sick, she waited for the next bomb to drop.

"I wasn't ready. Not even close, Daisy. I was in my senior year, with another year left to obtain my dual degrees. I'd already agreed to stay on at my uncle's ranch for three years after graduation. Her response was to accept a job in Helena."

"She left you?"

"Without a backward glance."

"I'm so sorry, Wyatt. What she did must've hurt you very much."

"Not as much as you'd think. If I'd loved Robyn, it should've hurt a lot more. Instead, I felt relief at not being pressured to do something I wasn't ready for."

"Do you still talk to her?"

"I haven't spoken to Robyn since she drove off with her graduate degree. The last I heard, she married a Helena banker, lived in town, and sold her horse." He chuckled on the last. "Are you ready for the walk home?"

Giving a brief nod, she stood, setting her cup on a tray before buttoning up her coat. His candid sharing of the relationship with Robyn stunned Daisy, making her realize how much she didn't know about Wyatt.

In contrast to his experience, she'd gone out with three men during college. None grew into more than good friendships. Even if he didn't love her, Wyatt's two-year relationship with Robyn meant a great deal to him.

Stepping into a snowstorm with stiff winds, Wyatt grabbed Daisy's arm. Drawing her back inside, he pulled out his phone, ordering a ride. It took thirty minutes before a car arrived to drive the short distance to her house.

Saving each other from slipping on the way inside, Wyatt shoved the door open, and almost fell on the floor. It took both of them to close it against winds that had increased to well over fifty miles per hour.

Stoking the fire in the living room, Daisy tossed on a couple extra logs. "How are you going to make it back to the ranch?"

"I'm not."

Slipping out of her coat, she tossed it over a chair. "No?'

"Is it okay if I sleep on your couch?"

"It's fine with me, but I doubt you'll fit. I have a guest room down the hall with a queen bed. You can sleep there."

Wyatt raised a brow. "Where's your bedroom?"

"Upstairs. If you snore, it won't bother me."

"I don't snore."

"Yeah, that's what all men say. I'll show you the bedroom." Pulling the pink beanie with golden poppies off her head, Daisy walked to the last room down the hall.

"This is it." The combination ceiling light and fan shone down on the bed with a gorgeous handmade quilt spread out on top. A green leather chair was positioned in a corner beside an antique dresser.

"What's with all the antiques? I pictured you as more modern."

"Mom would buy something whenever there was extra money, which wasn't often. I grew to appreciate them. Each piece has a history. If you listen, you might hear them telling their story."

Chuckling, he reached out, grabbed her around the waist, and hauled her to him. "I'd rather hear your story." Leaning down, he pressed his mouth to hers, feeling the heat to the tips of his toes. By the time he lifted his head, both were breathing heavily.

Kissing her once more, he straightened. "I could kiss you for hours." *Forever*, he thought, before pushing the idea aside. They barely knew each other.

Sure, they'd been friends in high school and gone out a few times. They'd always had a great time, and he'd missed her more than he'd imagined.

Eight years could make a huge difference in a person. He'd expected Daisy not to be the same woman he'd left to attend Montana State. Wyatt thought they'd get together a few times before his interest faded. It hadn't worked out that way. He wanted more time with her, not less.

Hands clasped together, Daisy rocked on her heels. "Are you ready to go to bed now, or do you want to watch a movie?" She hoped it was the latter.

"A movie. But none of that chick stuff."

Taking his hand, she headed back down the hall to the living room. "I have several streaming subscriptions. If you want to pick something, I'll make hot chocolate."

By the time she returned, the lights were lowered and Wyatt had selected a western she'd watched several times.

"Hope this one is all right with you."

"Are you kidding? Who doesn't love John Wayne?" Placing the mugs of hot chocolate on the coffee table, she sat down on the opposite end of the sofa from Wyatt.

Chuckling, he patted the area next to him. "Is there a reason you're all the way over there?"

Scooting beside him, he placed an arm over her shoulders, tucking her into his side. "That's a lot better." Pressing play, both relaxed as the movie started.

It didn't take long before his fingers moved over her shoulder and down her arm. Even through the sweater, she felt the heat, and assumed he did as well. No one had ever affected her to such a degree. Daisy doubted any man ever would. The thought excited and troubled her. She wouldn't trade their time together for anything. Right here, with this man, was where she wanted to be.

When he pressed a kiss to her temple, she sighed, snuggling closer. Half an hour into the movie, she yawned, her eyes fluttering. She didn't want to fall asleep during their first movie night together.

As it happened, the choice was taken from her. Hours later, she awoke, cradled in Wyatt's arms. She wanted nothing more than to stay there, both needed a good night's rest, which meant real beds.

"Wyatt, are you awake?"

"Hmmm?"

Grinning, she kissed his jaw. "Are you awake?"

Groaning, an eye popped open at his groggy voice. "No."

"You may want to head to the bedroom so you don't wake up with cramped muscles." Sitting up, she swung her legs over his inert body. "I'm going upstairs. Do you want anything before I head up?"

Several seconds passed before he answered. "You, Daiz. I just want you."

Chapter Twenty

The storm hadn't moved on when Daisy left her bed the following morning. Plodding into the bathroom, she brushed her teeth before showering and slipping into a yellow sweater and denim overalls with an embroidered sunflower smack in the center of the front pocket.

Braiding her hair, she slipped into yellow socks to match her sweater before grabbing her favorite Sorel wedge snow boots. Checking the mirror, she smiled. It was one of her favorite outfits.

A gust of wind slammed against the upstairs windows, causing her to place a steadying hand on her dresser. Waiting until the gusts stopped, she took the stairs to the first floor. The door to the guest room was closed tight, indicating Wyatt still slept.

A quick look outside confirmed his truck was still parked at the curb. It would take a good deal of shoveling for Wyatt to get on the road.

Making a cup of coffee, she sipped it while frying half a pound of bacon. Keeping the slices warm, she fixed hash browns, deciding to hold off on the eggs until Wyatt joined her.

At almost six in the morning, she would've expected him to be up and about. As the thought crossed her mind, she heard the door open and boots hit the hardwood floors.

"Morning, Daisy." He didn't hesitate to grip her shoulders for a deep, lingering kiss. When finished, he lifted his head, satisfied with the look on her face. She was no more immune to his kisses than he was of hers.

Reaching behind her, he picked up a slice of bacon, taking a bite. "This is great. Are we having eggs with the hash browns?"

"Yes, and stop stealing our breakfast. Make some coffee while I finish."

"Yes, ma'am." Sneaking another slice of bacon while she pulled eggs from the refrigerator, he finished it before making coffee.

"Fried or scrambled? By the way, I saw you take more bacon." The comment was said with a smile. "Should I cook more?"

"Depends on if you want any. Fried would be fine. Over easy."

Adding a pat of butter to the bacon grease, she glanced over her shoulder at him. "One or two?"

"Five would be great."

Whirling around, she set her hands on her hips. "Five?"

"Is that too many? I have that many at home."

She opened the carton, relaxing at the sight of seven eggs. "Five over easy eggs coming up. Do you mind putting bread in the toaster? There's wheat and sourdough."

"How many slices do you want?"

"One, and I'd like sourdough. There's jam in the refrigerator. Homemade marionberry and blackberry. Honey's in the cupboard."

"You made the jam?"

Flipping the eggs, she slid them on a plate, along with hash browns and the rest of the bacon. "Surprised?" Handing him the plate, she started her eggs. "Go ahead and eat before yours get cold."

"I'm learning all kinds of things about you, Daisy Raines. One of them is you have a domestic streak. Cooking, sewing, decorating. I guess the last shouldn't surprise me since you own an art shop."

Basting the eggs, she scooped them onto her plate, joining him in the dining room. "Growing up, there wasn't money for store bought clothes. Mom made everything until I was old enough to sew. Then we both made our clothes, or found them at the thrift shop. We reworked the used clothing to make them look different. For a long time, I saw it as a game. By fourteen, I realized used clothes were a necessity. We became pretty clever at customizing everything. I still buy some of my clothes at the thrift shop."

Digging into her food, she took several bites before feeling his gaze on her. "What? Is the food not okay?"

"The food is great." *You're great,* he wanted to say. "Did I tell you about the injured dog Virgil and I found at the ranch?"

"No. What happened?"

"We're not sure. Virgil and Doc Worrel found bite marks on her. We think it might've been a wolf. They required sutures."

Daisy said nothing about Dorie, although she felt the sting of seeing her with Wyatt at the restaurant. He'd explained what happened, yet the sense of betrayal still bothered her. She had to find a way to let it go.

"Will she recover?"

"Dorie thinks so. Virgil's going to be watching over her."

Reaching out, she grabbed a piece of his bacon. "It's a shame he never attended veterinary school. He'd make a great doctor."

Wyatt's jaw tightened as he thought of his father's failure to do as he'd promised. "I'm still hoping we'll find a way for him to attend vet school in Colorado, Washington, or Oregon. I don't know the real reason Pop didn't fulfill his promise to Virgil. I'm determined to make it right."

"What about loans or grants?"

Pushing his empty plate away, he crossed his arms. "Whatever is needed. Virgil was born to be a doctor, and not just for animals."

Daisy knew what he meant. Virgil was born to work with people or animals. "He's one of the most talented men I've ever known."

Without responding, he shoved his chair back to stalk toward the front windows. "Nothing's changed outside. I can't see past the edge of the porch."

"I'll check the weather report." Daisy pulled out her phone, seeing zero bars. "Do you have service?"

Looking at his phone, he shook his head. "No. Wouldn't tell me much more than I can see." Turning toward her, his smile shot straight to her heart. "Neither of us are going anywhere for a while. What do you want to do?"

"Do?"

One brow lifted. "To kill time until the storm passes." Grabbing his chair, he turned it around to straddle it, resting his arms on the back.

His first choice would be to take her into his arms and kiss her senseless. Wyatt didn't know where this burning desire for Daisy came from. Yes, she was beautiful and smart, with a big heart. Unlike some people, she had goals and worked to attain them. He enjoyed his time with her, looked forward to seeing her again. He loved holding and kissing her, couldn't wait to do it again.

Still, there were a lot of beautiful women in Brilliance. Most of them smart, with goals. He'd probably enjoy spending time with any number of them. Not one piqued his interest.

The quirky blonde who often preferred driving her vintage VW bug to her almost new GMC Acadia, wore overalls with an embroidered sunflower, and pink sweaters with teapots, occupied his mind.

Daisy intrigued him more than any woman he'd ever known. Much more so than Robyn, a woman he thought he'd loved.

"I suppose we could watch another movie. Or I could show you my plans for expanding my shop." Her head rose so her eyes met his.

"Can I kiss you while we're reviewing your plans?" He watched as her neck and cheeks colored.

"That's a fabulous idea. Although, it might take a great deal longer to explain what I hope to do."

Standing, he took her hand. "Show me the plans and I'll take care of the rest."

"Where is my son?" Anson stalked about his office, his blood pressure rising. Stopping, his steel gray eyes locked on Virgil. "Well? Where is he?" His voice rose with each word, his face turning a blotchy purple.

"My guess is the storm has him stranded in town. There's no phone service or he would've called."

Anson slammed a fist onto his desk. "He's with that no good Raines woman, isn't he?"

"I don't know."

Anson moved to within inches of Virgil, who refused to flinch or show any amount of weakness. "She's not the right woman for him. The same as that Cardoza woman isn't right for you."

Hands clenched at his sides, Virgil's jaw clenched.

"Nothing to say, Redstar?"

"There's nothing to say. You already know I broke it off with Lily eight years ago."

Whirling around, Anson paced away, anger rolling off him in waves. "I'll disown him if he's with her," he shouted.

"Anson, what's going on?" Margie stepped into the office, walking up to him. "You need to calm down."

"It's that son of yours. He's with that woman in town. I'll disown him for going against my wishes!"

"You'll do no such thing. Sit down and stop shouting. Virgil, please ask Nacho to fix tea for my husband."

"Yes, ma'am."

When the door closed, Margie pointed to a nearby chair. "Sit down, Anson. You're going to have another heart attack if you don't get your anger under control."

"Leave me alone, Margie. It's my home and I'll do as I please. Our son will ruin his life if he continues on with her."

"Whether he's with Daisy or not is Wyatt's decision. Do you want to alienate your son over his choice of women?"

"If he marries her, he'll never be allowed back on the ranch. Never, Margie. Do you understand me?"

"I understand you've an irrational dislike of Daisy and it's going to tear this family apart if you don't let it go."

Jumping up, he glared down at her. "When he returns, I'll make it clear he's not to see her again. I expect you to back me up on this, Margie."

Walking to the window, she stared out at the continuing storm, taking deep breaths to cool her own growing frustration. Knowing her husband would have another heart attack if he continued, she turned slowly to face him.

"You have to stop this, Anson. I won't have you ruining Wyatt's future because your father ruined yours."

Taking a few feet toward her, he glared at Margie. "I don't know what you're talking about."

Pacing away, she wrapped both arms around her waist. She'd carried the knowledge inside for their entire marriage. Perhaps now was the time to let the truth out.

"I've always known you loved Daisy's mother."

"I never—"

"Stop, Anson. We've lived without the truth for too long."

Deflated, he lowered himself into a chair. "How did you find out?"

"Everyone in town knew you loved her mother, planned to marry her after she graduated from high school. Your father stepped in and forbade you to marry her. The story is you came to blows, threatened to leave the ranch and run away with her."

Walking to the window, she again looked out, seeing little of the ranch, which had been her home for close to thirty years. Margie loved the land, what they'd accomplished. Over time, she believed Anson had come to love her.

"He used all the same arguments you're using with Wyatt. I'm sure there's a part of you who thinks Daisy should've been your child. But she isn't. You gave in to your father, walked away from love, and married me."

"Margie..."

"Let me finish. It wasn't easy knowing you didn't love me. Still, we have three incredible boys. Sons who will carry on the legacy of Whistle Rock Ranch. *If* you don't interfere. You have to let the past go, Anson. Wyatt must be allowed to make the choice taken from you all those years ago. He loves Daisy, and that girl loves him with all her heart. You either back away and let those two make up their own minds, or I'm leaving."

Panic shown in his bloodshot eyes. "You don't mean that."

"I've never meant anything more. You made sure I had my own savings, for which I'm grateful. I'll use it to start a new life if you don't come to your senses."

Chapter Twenty-One

Virgil stood outside the office, frozen in place by Margie's declaration. Anson Bonner had loved Daisy's mother, and his own father had forbidden him from marrying her. History was repeating itself. The sense of it eluded Virgil.

He felt sick for Margie. A fine woman who'd gone through life knowing her husband might never love her. A wife who'd stood by her husband through hard times and illness, giving him three wonderful sons. He wondered if his father knew the story.

Knocking on the already open door, he took a step inside. "I have Anson's tea."

"Thank you, Virgil. Please set it down on the table."

Placing it near Anson, he tried not to notice the stricken look and green tinge to his skin. "Is there anything else you need?"

"I believe we're fine. Do you mind closing the door when you leave?"

"Not at all. I'll be in the apartment if you need anything."

Closing the door behind him, he slipped into his coat and gloves, willing the storm to end. He wanted to call Wyatt, warn him about his father's mood.

Instead of leaving out the front door, he walked through the house to the kitchen. A rope had been attached between the outside kitchen door and the bunkhouse years earlier. It was meant for storms such as this, allowing people to move from one building to the other without getting lost in the whiteout.

Virgil put one hand over the other, making his way to the bunkhouse. He hadn't decided whether or not to say anything of what he'd heard to his best friend. It wasn't his place to pass along a private conversation between a wife and her husband.

Virgil did know he'd say nothing to his father. Jasper and Anson were tight. Whatever he told him would be passed along to Anson within an hour.

Walking through the main bunkhouse to the door leading to the apartment, he noticed most of the men reclined on their beds. Some read, others wrote letters, a few slept. Barrel sat on the edge of his bed working on a piece of leather. At his feet lay Trooper, still recovering from the attack.

These were men not used to sitting around. They were born to be outside, handling the duties of a successful, working ranch.

"How's Trooper doing?"

Setting aside the leather, Barrel bent down, running a hand over the dog's head and neck. "Pretty good given what happened. No infection, which is a relief."

"Golden labs are a tough dog. She'll be a good addition to the ranch. I'll be in the apartment if you need me."

"Will do, boss."

"You do realize I'm not your boss."

"Wyatt and you are what make this ranch run. It's your ideas and hard work that make it successful. So, yeah. You're my boss."

Giving a slow nod, Virgil entered the apartment. Jasper slept on his bed, his breathing labored. He used the inhaler almost every day, which seemed often. Virgil planned to call the doctor once the storm ended and phone service was available.

Sitting at the small table, he once again considered what he'd heard. Margie's comment about Anson believing Daisy should've been his daughter stuck with Virgil. If that were true, he could understand why Anson wouldn't be inclined to have her marry his son. Daisy would be a constant reminder of what he'd lost.

What didn't make sense was all the times he'd seen Anson look at Margie with what to Virgil appeared to be love. There'd been dozens of instances over the years when he'd taken his wife's hand, holding it against his chest. If he didn't love Margie when they married, Anson had come to love her over their years together.

Stretching out on his bed, an idea came to Virgil. A way to possibly make Wyatt aware of what he'd heard without breaking any confidences. He'd think about it a little longer before making a final decision. Hearing hail pelt the windows, and though it was the middle of the day, he closed his eyes.

The almost nap wasn't long. Virgil didn't sleep as he pondered different ideas on how to approach Margie.

Swinging his legs to the floor, he scrubbed both hands over his face before looking outside. The storm appeared to be slowing. He could see the main house for the first time since the blizzard began.

Tugging his phone from a pocket, he saw three bars. Punching in the number, he waited.

"Virgil. How is it at the ranch?"

"Storm is slowing, Wyatt. Where are you?"

"Daisy's house. I should be on the road in a few minutes. Anything I should know?"

"Is Daisy close by?"

"She's upstairs. What's going on?"

"Anson's on a rampage. You're the focus of his rage."

"Because I'm not at the ranch?"

"Because he believes you're with Daisy."

Wyatt groaned, tired of his father's interference. "Though it's not his business, he's right."

"Be aware he's in one of his moods, and tread carefully. I'm heading to the house now. Having me there might help."

"Thanks, Virgil. I'll see you soon."

"Be careful, Wyatt. The roads are bound to be a mess."

Walking to his father's bed, he noticed Jasper breathed easier than a couple hours earlier. Not wanting to wake him, Virgil put on his coat, gloves, and hat before leaving out the back door.

Entering the main house through the kitchen, he came to an abrupt stop. Working next to Nacho was a woman of about thirty. Sitting a few feet away from them was a boy of no more than eight. Closing the door, he brushed snow off his coat.

"Nacho. Did you pick up an assistant during the storm?"

"Margie thinks I need help." He nodded to the woman. "This one arrived just before the blizzard."

Ignoring Nacho's sour expression, he smiled at her. "I'm Virgil Redstar."

Offering a tentative smile, she met his gaze. "Emma Griffin." She nodded toward the boy, her smile brightening. "This is my son, Koa."

"It's good to meet you both. How old are you, Koa?"

Looking up from the book in his lap, he shot a look at his mother, who nodded. "I'm eight."

"Then you're almost a man."

Features solemn, his voice turned serious. "Mama says I'm the man of our family."

"Is that so? Well, I'm certain you'll do a fine job. Nacho, do you know where Margie is?"

"Last I knew, she was in her study."

Looking at Emma, he touched the brim of his hat. "Ma'am."

Margie's study was linked to Anson's office with a connecting door. She sat behind her desk, staring at a paper in front of her.

"Do you have a minute?"

Raising her head, she set the paper aside. "Of course. Sit down and start talking."

Virgil laughed at the phrase Margie used since he and Wyatt were young. "When I brought the tea for Anson, I overheard some of your conversation."

"I see. How much did you hear?"

Mouth twisting into a grimace, he lowered his voice. "I know about his feelings for Daisy's mother."

Letting out a breath, she stared down at her hands. "So you heard most of what I said."

"Yes. A good deal. The door was open."

"Don't worry about it, Virgil. There are many people in town and a few here at the ranch who know of his feelings for her."

"It helps clarify why he doesn't want Wyatt and Daisy together."

"I agree. Have you said anything to Wyatt?"

"Only that his father was on a rampage. But I do think Wyatt should know."

Standing, Margie walked to the window without responding. "The storm seems to have weakened. I see the men have gone back to work. Nacho told me the forecast is for a few days of clear skies." Turning from the window, she couldn't hide her distress. "Talking about Anson's love for Daisy's mother is difficult for me."

"It's obvious he loves you. Whatever he felt for her died a long time ago."

"Anson says the same. Most days, I believe him. There are times, such as today, when his anger about Daisy makes me wonder if he ever did get over her mother."

"Would it bother you if Wyatt and Daisy got married?"

A genuine smile curved Margie's mouth. "Not at all. She's a wonderful young woman. I hope Anson doesn't scare Wyatt off."

Chuckling, Virgil shook his head. "I doubt anyone can scare Wyatt away from Daisy. If they stop seeing each other, it will be their choice, not pressure from Anson."

"I hope you're right." Sitting back down, she leaned forward, resting her arms on the desk. "So you think Wyatt should know about Anson's relationship with Daisy's mother?"

"I do. It's going to come out sometime. I'm certain Wyatt would rather hear it from you."

Daisy followed Wyatt as far as her shop, lighthearted and excited about where their relationship may go. He'd invited her and Lily to Thanksgiving at the ranch. A quick call to her friend confirmed they'd attend. A surprise, since Daisy assumed Lily would prefer to stay away from Virgil.

Although mid-afternoon, she decided to open the shop for a few hours. Cleaning the sidewalk of snow and bookkeeping could fill her time between what she expected to be few customers.

"Was that Wyatt Bonner's truck parked outside your house all night?"

Stopping the task of shoveling snow, Daisy straightened to see Lydia, the owner of Brilliance Coffee and Bakery, holding a white bag.

"He couldn't get out of town until a little bit ago. It was fortunate I'd changed the sheets in the guest room. What do you have in the bag?"

Holding it up, Lydia handed it to Daisy. "Bear claws, and cheese Danish for Wyatt. I couldn't get to the shop to open it until an hour ago, so everything was a day old. Thought I'd hand them out around town. Your bag is the last of them."

"That's wonderful of you. Thanks for including me and Wyatt. Do you have time to come inside?"

"Unfortunately, there was a leak in my basement. I'm meeting a plumber there in twenty minutes. Another time?"

"Whenever is good for you." Daisy considered her next question, deciding to ask. "Were you in town when my father was here?"

"I was. They made a fine couple. Your mother deserved happiness, especially after Anson Bonner's father forced him to stop seeing her."

Daisy stared wide-eyed at Lydia, her throat tight. "My mother and Wyatt's father?"

"I'm so sorry. I thought you knew. Most everyone in town knew Anson dated your mother for months. We expected them to marry, but his father forced Anson to end it. Your mother took the breakup very hard. I honestly thought your mother or someone else would've told you, Daisy. I feel horrible."

"Don't, Lydia. It's not your fault. My mother should've said something."

"Does she know you're seeing Wyatt?"

Letting out a sigh, she shook her head. "No. They've been traveling overseas. I planned to tell her after they returned. Who knows? By then, Anson might convince Wyatt to stop seeing me."

"Don't think that way. Anson was never as strong as Wyatt. He's not going to back down the way his father did." Reaching out, Lydia touched Daisy's arm. "You two are meant for each other. Trust in Wyatt, as he'll do what's right."

Chapter Twenty-Two

Daisy sat cross-legged on the living room floor, surrounded by shoe boxes of various sizes. Her mother had labeled each one with dates and contents, making the search a little easier.

The problem was Daisy couldn't locate even one of her mother's journals. No matter how tired she was from working two jobs, she wrote in her journal every night before bed.

"Did she take them with her to Florida?" Daisy asked herself, frustrated at the lack of progress.

If what Lydia said was true, the journal would've been dated soon after her mother graduated from high school. Rubbing her forehead, Daisy tried to remember all the hiding places her mother used for birthday and Christmas presents. Then it came to her.

Jumping up, she almost tripped on the shoe boxes in her rush to get upstairs. Taking the steps two at a time, Daisy hurried to the last bedroom down the hall.

Other than to clean, she hadn't been in the room for months. Still, she could remember every inch of it. Ignoring the two night stands and dresser, she opened the closet door.

Small by most standards, her mother used it to store summer clothes in the winter, and winter clothes each summer. It was also her favorite place to hide presents. Was it also where she hid her journals?

Grabbing a chair, Daisy used it to reach a box on the top shelf. Heavier than expected, she steadied herself before turning toward the bed. She'd gotten within a foot of it when her toe caught on the throw rug, propelling her and the contents of the box onto the quilted spread. There, in front of her, were at least two dozen brown leather journals.

With a shout of excitement, Daisy grabbed one after another, creating piles by date. Finishing, she picked up four journals, starting with her mother's senior year of high school.

Holding them against her chest, she went straight to the kitchen. A large pot of tea would be the perfect companion to get her through her mother's private thoughts.

Heating the water, Daisy experienced a twinge of guilt. The journals, and what they contained, didn't belong to her. Reading them would be a clear invasion of privacy.

As she waited for the water to boil, Daisy considered what to do. Of the few choices, the best option would be to call her mother. They'd always been close. Perhaps not so much now, with her mother and stepfather traveling a good part of each year.

Taking her tea and journals to the dining room, she set the books aside. The thought of opening any of them no longer held the same appeal. Not without her mother's knowledge.

With that thought, she had her answer. Sliding her phone from a pocket, she checked the time before calling her mother. Waiting as it rang, she splayed a hand over her churning stomach. Twice, she almost hung up, realizing she hadn't planned what to say.

"Did you ever date Anson Bonner?"

"I heard you used to go out with Anson Bonner."

"Why didn't you ever tell me about Anson Bonner?"

Not one sounded right. She should've thought this through before calling.

"Are you there, Daisy?"

"Mom? Are you in Florida?"

"We returned a few days ago after two months away. It was all so fantastic. You have to travel with us sometime. How are you?"

"Wonderful. The shop is doing spectacular. I've signed two new artists in the last week."

"I'm so proud of you, Daisy. I always knew the shop would be a big success. Are you seeing anyone?"

"As in dating?"

"Of course I mean dating. Is there anyone special since we last talked?"

Hesitating, she let out a breath. "I'm seeing Wyatt Bonner. You remember him, right?"

"I do remember him. The two of you dated before he left for college." It may have been Daisy's imagination, but all the joy seemed to have left her mother's voice. "Is he working at the ranch?"

"Yes. In fact, his father has handed over a great deal of the responsibilities to Wyatt."

"I knew it would happen at some point, but it seems a little soon. Was there a reason?"

"Yes." Daisy's throat tightened. "Anson had a heart attack a few months ago. They almost lost him."

Several beats passed before she answered, her voice shaky. "Will he be all right?"

"If he behaves."

"He never was one to stay within the lines."

Mouth drawing into a thin line, Daisy blew out a slow breath. "Mom, there's something I have to ask you."

"All right."

"Did you date Anson Bonner?"

As the silence stretched, she wondered if her mother planned to answer. "Mom, did you hear me?"

"Yes, I heard."

"I'll understand if you don't want to tell me."

"It's not that, Daisy."

"I'm sorry, Mom. Forget I asked."

"No, you should know about it. It's been such a long time. We dated for two years before Anson's father forced him to break it off. We loved each other so much. He asked me to marry him, and I said yes. The breakup hurt me deeply. A year later, he married Margie. Seeing them together...well, it almost killed me. All of this is not a secret. Many in town witnessed what happened. Why ask about this now?"

"Anson hates me."

"What reason could he have for hating you?"

"I hardly know him."

"The older Anson gets, the more he's like his father. Dictatorial, bullying people to get his way. But to hate you is unacceptable. Do you care about Wyatt?"

"Very much. Perhaps too much."

"All I can tell you is to keep seeing Wyatt. Don't let Anson scare you off."

"It's not really up to me. Wyatt may give in to his father's demands."

"Not if he truly wants to be with you, Daisy. If he doesn't, then you're better off without him."

"This should be the last one." Wyatt pulled the wire tight while Virgil secured it, both men stepping back to double-check their work.

They'd worked for almost four hours on the south side of the ranch while Barrel and a few other men repaired the fences to the north. Tomorrow would be their first full day after the storm, and they were more than ready to eat and turn in for the night.

So far, Wyatt had avoided his father, and his mother. Although the last was unintentional.

"That's it for tonight, Wyatt." Virgil clasped him on the back before picking up the tools.

"Great, because I'm starving. Do you think Nacho saved anything for us?"

"If not, we'll figure something out. The two large refrigerators are always overflowing with food."`

Wyatt and Virgil sat at the large kitchen table, talking about how the storm affected the ranch while finishing plates filled with leftovers. Neither had come inside until almost eight, determined to fix most of the damaged fence.

"What's going on with Pop?" Wyatt relaxed, finishing a bottle of water. He assumed his father vented about him being stuck in town and not at the ranch. Control freak didn't begin to define the man.

"You need to speak with Margie."

"I will, but give me the short version."

"Daisy."

Stiffening, Wyatt sat up, his jaw tight. "Who I see is none of his business."

"I know that, but Anson refuses to accept he has no say on who you date."

"What'd he say?"

"Margie asked me to fix tea for Anson to calm him down. When I returned, his office door was open. I didn't hear the entire conversation. You need to speak with Margie.”

“No better time than now.” Almost tipping over his chair in his hurry to find his mother, Wyatt headed to her office. Finding the light still on, he gave a light tap on the door before entering.

“Well, it’s about time you came to say hello.” Standing, she rounded the desk to give him a hug. “How are you?”

“Virgil said I needed to speak with you about Pop’s rant today. What’s going on?”

“Sit down. This will take a few minutes.” Lowering herself into one of the easy chairs, she waited while Wyatt sat in the one next to her.

“How is Pop?”

“He went up to our bedroom early. I’m hoping he’s asleep. I can’t believe how worked up he is about you seeing Daisy. It’s irrational, and will lead to another heart attack if he doesn’t learn to control his anger.”

“And stop trying to control my life.”

Sighing, she nodded. “He’s obsessed with pressuring you to stop seeing her.”

“Why does he care?”

“I wondered the same. After today’s unreasonable reaction, I’m certain of the reason.” Clasping her hands in her lap, Margie let out a ragged breath.

“Anson and Daisy’s mother dated years ago.”

His brows scrunched together in confusion, though he didn’t comment.

"They were just out of high school. From what I know, they were truly in love. Anson asked her to marry him, and she accepted. When his father found out, he threatened to kick him off the ranch and disinherit him. Anson refused, but your grandfather continued to pressure him. I don't know how long it took or what else his father threatened, but Anson broke the engagement."

Closing her eyes, she sat silent for several long moments before continuing.

"I found out later your grandfather and my mother had already discussed matching me up with Anson. We married a year later. I always knew he didn't love me." She choked out a strangled laugh.

"I'll get you water."

She waved Wyatt off. "I knew his decision to marry me had almost destroyed Daisy's mother. I've regretted my marriage to Anson more times than I can count. If it weren't for you boys, I would've left long ago."

"But you stayed. Why?"

"An excellent question without a good answer. Once I became pregnant, my chance to leave disappeared. The years blended together as I became entrenched in family activities, school functions, and sports. Anson and I rarely saw each other during the day. By the time he came to bed, I was usually asleep. I didn't agree with him sending you to your uncle's. Now I understand, and am glad you had a chance to get away. You learned a great deal from Emmett and Lucinda. The inheritance from your grandfather gives you options your father didn't have."

"Where does his hatred for Daisy come from?"

"Did you ever notice how much Daisy looks like her mother?"

Wyatt's head dipped before he rubbed a hand over his mouth. "I never thought about it."

"Trust me. Daisy is the spitting image of her mother. If you two ever get serious and marry, you'll be living at the ranch."

"And Pop would be forced to see her every day."

"A reminder of what he gave up."

Shredding fingers through his hair, he stalked to the window, looking out at a sky dotted with millions of stars. A different sight than twenty-four hours earlier. Walking back to his mother, Wyatt knelt down in front of her, taking her hands in his.

"Pop loves you, Mom. Anyone can see it when he looks at you."

"He does now. The first ten years were the most difficult. He often talked about her in his sleep. All that stopped by the time Jonah was born. I believe Anson's love for his sons helped him fall in love with me."

Squeezing her hands, Wyatt rose, not sure what else to say. He didn't want to be controlled by anyone, especially his overbearing father.

"I won't give up Daisy."

Margie's eyes widened. "You're in love with her?"

"I'm not sure it's love, but I care about her a great deal. She's a good person, Mom. Kind, talented, and always cheerful. Her business is a great success, and she plans to expand. I want to see where this relationship goes.”

“Does she feel the same?”

A smile curved his mouth. “Yes.”

“Then stay strong. Don’t let Anson bully you into giving her up. Trust me. He’ll come at you with everything he has.” Standing, she walked back to her desk. “I’ve already told him I’ll leave if he doesn’t stop harassing you.”

“I’m sure that went over well.”

This earned a chuckle from Margie. “I meant it, Wyatt. I’m tired of him using his money and power to force people into decisions which benefit him. You have the education, experience, and resources to carve your own path. I don’t want you to leave, but I’ll support whatever you decide.”

Chapter Twenty-Three

"What do you plan to take to the Bonners' for Thanksgiving dinner? We are going, right?" Lily sat on the floor in Daisy's living room, sipping hot chocolate while reviewing the list of businesses who'd agreed to offer the calendars.

"If you're certain about being around Virgil, then yes, I'd like to go." Daisy knew she should call and confirm they were still invited. She'd planned to ask Wyatt, but he hadn't been in touch since leaving when the storm cleared enough for him to leave.

"Have you heard from Wyatt?"

"Not since he left after the storm." Daisy joined Lily on the floor. "I'll call Margie."

"Why not call Wyatt?"

Holding the mug to her mouth, she blew across it before taking a swallow. The drink warmed her, helped settle what had been bothering her all week.

"Did you know my mother dated Anson Bonner?"

Lily almost dropped her mug, moving fast to hold onto it. "Are you sure?"

"I called my mom, and she confirmed it."

"Geez. Who would've thought? He's been married to Margie forever." Setting her mug down, Lily studied Daisy.

"It was right after high school. They dated for two years before his father forced him to break up with her."

"So it runs in the family."

Picking up the list of businesses, Daisy scanned the pages. "What?"

"Using intimidation to get what they want."

"Mom was devastated. He married Margie a year later. A year, Lily. Anson must not have loved Mom very much."

"Does Wyatt know about your mom and his dad?"

Dropping the list into her lap, she shook her head. "I have no idea. We need to talk soon."

"Probably a good idea. So, what are you taking to the Bonners'?"

"I don't know."

"Daisy, it's three days away. You need to make a decision." Lily's voice hovered on panic, a rare occurrence.

"Are you sure you're all right going to the ranch? You're acting a little odd."

"Because I want time to plan what I'm taking?"

"Never mind. Maybe I'm the one acting weird. It's just that Wyatt and I have been talking and texting every day since we started seeing each other."

"And you've heard nothing."

Daisy gave a slow nod. "Yeah. For about a week. Maybe Anson already got to him."

Grabbing Daisy's phone from the coffee table, searching for Margie's number, Lily called before handing the phone to her. "Ask Margie if we're still invited."

Putting it to her ear, she felt her stomach clench as she waited. After several rings, she began composing a message. "Hi, Margie. It's Daisy."

"Haven't heard from you in a while. How are you?"

"Good. Hey, Wyatt invited me and Lily to your Thanksgiving dinner. I wanted to double-check to make sure it's all right if we join you."

"We'd love to have you and Lily. Don't worry about bringing anything. Nacho and his new assistant already have way too much food planned."

"If you're sure."

"Absolutely. Arrive around three. We'll eat about four."

"Thank you, Margie. We're looking forward to seeing you."

"And Wyatt, I hope."

Before Daisy could respond, Margie ended the call.

"Are we going?"

Still thinking about Margie's comment, she pursed her lips, and nodded. "Yes. She said we didn't need to bring anything."

Rising from her spot on the floor, Lily stretched, rolling her head from side to side. "I think we should bring something."

"I agree. I'd be embarrassed to arrive empty-handed. Do you remember the bread pudding I made for our open house last winter? Or the chocolate buttermilk pie we had for the summer picnic?"

Lily tapped a finger against her lips. "Do I have to make a choice? They're both spectacular."

"How about you come over here Wednesday after your shift and we'll make both?"

"I get off at six. Should I go by the grocery and get what we need?"

"Just come straight here. One of my clerks will be working Wednesday. I'll be able to get to the store early." Clasping her hands together, a broad smile spread across Daisy's face. "This is going to be a perfect Thanksgiving."

Wyatt never called before Daisy and Lily loaded the desserts into the SUV on Thursday afternoon for the trip to Whistle Rock Ranch. She'd sent him three texts, one each day, never hearing back from Wyatt.

The lack of communication bothered Daisy. She told herself it meant nothing. They were still a couple, and he knew she and Lily would join them for dinner. What if she was wrong?

She and Lily had taken special care with their clothes, hair, and makeup. Instead of a long, flowing skirt, she wore heavy leggings, a knee length black pencil skirt, tall boots, and black sweater with a plaid vest, and a string of pearls showcasing one of her custom made pendants. Lily wore wool slacks with matching sweater, ankle boots, and jewelry Daisy had given her on her last birthday. She dared Anson to find fault in their attire.

Parking as close to the house as possible, each took a dessert, stomping their boots on the plank porch before knocking. Voices and music came from inside. By the number of cars, it appeared quite a few people from town had been invited.

When no one answered, Daisy tried the handle. It turned easily.

The living room was filled with at least forty people, most talking in small groups.

She spotted Wyatt between the living and dining rooms with Dorie on one side of him and a woman she didn't recognize on the other. He threw back his head, laughing at something Dorie had said.

"Don't read anything into him being with Dorie," Lily said. "Let's get the desserts into the kitchen and join everyone."

"Hello, Lily. Daisy." Both turned at Virgil's voice. "Can I help you with your plates?"

"We're fine. On our way to the kitchen," Daisy answered.

"I'll go with you. Nacho isn't in the best of moods today. Plus, I want to introduce you to his new assistant."

"When I called to confirm Lily and I would be attending, Margie mentioned an assistant. What do you think of him?"

"It's a woman, and so far, she seems to be more than competent. Emma Griffin. Single mom with an eight-year-old son. Don't ask about the boy's father because I have no information."

Daisy felt a pang of disappointment when Wyatt never took his gaze from Dorie. He looked striking in black jeans and boots, a dark plaid shirt, and exquisite bolo tie. Beside him, Dorie could've been a model rather than the town vet. Perhaps she'd been wrong about him not having an interest in the stunning doctor.

Setting the desserts where Nacho indicated, Daisy introduced herself to the new employee. "I'd love to come back to the kitchen in a bit and learn more about you and your son."

"I'm not going anywhere, Daisy. I'd like to learn more about your shop."

"You know about it?"

"Wyatt can't stop talking about you and how talented you are." Emma leaned toward Daisy, lowering her voice. "He's in love with you."

"How would you know?"

Emma smiled. "It wasn't hard. He and his father have been arguing about your relationship all week. Both have a tendency to shout when they're angry. I hope he doesn't leave."

"Leave?"

"Emma, I need your help over here." Nacho's order stopped any reply.

"I'd better go. Nice meeting you, Daisy."

"We'll talk again, Emma."

Leaving the kitchen, she noticed Lily and Virgil apart from the rest of the guests. Whatever they were saying seemed strained. At least they were talking, which was a start.

"How long have you been here?" Wyatt's deep voice washed over her an instant before lips pressed against her temple. "You should've found me."

"You were talking with others and I had dessert to put in the kitchen."

Taking her hand, he led her into his mother's study, closing the door behind them. Without a word, he turned her toward him, covering her mouth with his.

It wasn't a short or soft kiss. He plundered her mouth, exploring, encouraging until the heat created became too intense.

"I've missed you, Daisy."

"And I've missed you. More than you can imagine." Taking a small step back, she took his hand in hers. "Is everything all right?"

"Fine. Why?"

"This may not be a good time."

"Not a good time for what, Daisy?"

Pacing away, she stood by the window for long moments before Wyatt rested his hands on her waist. "What's bothering you, sweetheart?"

"When I didn't hear from you for over a week, I thought your father had gotten to you."

"Gotten to me?"

"The way your grandfather persuaded your father to stop seeing my mother."

Turning her to face him, he gripped her shoulders. "You know about them?"

"I spoke to my mother a few days ago."

"My understanding is they were in love, planned to marry."

"Mom said your father ended the engagement when your grandfather threatened him. He married Margie a year later. It broke my mother's heart, Wyatt. Now Anson wants to do the same with us. I mean, I know we have no plans to marry, but when I didn't hear from you, I thought..."

"Look at me, Daisy." Cupping her face in his hands, he pressed a kiss to her lips. "Now, listen to me. My father has been on me to stop seeing you since I returned from your house last week. We've argued about it so often, I've lost count." Kissing her again, he sat down on a nearby chair.

"I'm sorry I didn't call, but I needed time to think. To make some decisions."

"About us?"

"About a lot of things, Daisy."

Her stomach clenched, knowing where this conversation was going. Wyatt had changed his mind about them. Wrapping her arms around her waist, she began moving to the door. She refused to let him see her tears when she learned his decision.

"I understand, Wyatt. You have a lot of responsibilities and so many wonderful plans. Your family needs you here. Your father needs you." She loved Wyatt so much, but refused to make this difficult on him. Forcing a smile, she stepped to the door, drawing it open. "It's better this way."

Realizing her intent, Wyatt jumped up, grabbing Daisy's arm, tugging her back into the study. "You aren't going anywhere until we've talked this through." Closing the door, he pulled her into his arms.

"I don't know what's going on in your pretty head, but I'm not letting you go."

Hope began to grow. "You aren't?"

"Not a chance, sweetheart. Sit down with me, and I'll tell you what I want."

Chapter Twenty-Four

"First, I made a huge discovery while working in freezing temperatures."

"What did you discover?"

Gripping Daisy's waist, Wyatt lifted her onto his lap. Raising her chin with a finger, he met her expectant gaze.

"I love you, Daisy Raines. I knew it when we rode up to Whistle Rock, but wasn't ready to face it. I'm ready now." Lowering his mouth, he captured hers in a searing kiss meant to lessen her concerns. Raising his head, he smiled, swiping a tear from her cheek. "Now, you're supposed to tell me you love me."

Choking out a laugh, she stroked his jaw. "I've loved you forever, Wyatt Bonner. But that doesn't change the fact your father hates me."

Letting out a deep sigh, Wyatt tightened his hold around her. "He doesn't hate you, Daisy. What he can't bear is how much you look like your mother. Pop knows that if we ever marry, you'll be living here with me."

"Marry?" Daisy had never allowed herself to even dream about a life with Wyatt.

"Truthfully, I haven't thought that far ahead, but I know my father has."

She glanced away, not wanting him to see her disappointment. He might care a great deal for her, maybe love her. Marriage would be a huge leap for a man like Wyatt Bonner.

"I'm right with you about anything permanent, cowboy." She kissed his jaw before relaxing into his embrace.

Frowning, he looked down into her face. Her response perplexed him. He knew she wanted to marry someday, have children and a real family. Everything she'd never had growing up.

"I never said I don't want to marry. Just that it's a little soon to consider now. It doesn't change the fact I love you, Daisy."

She needed to change the subject. "Is he threatening to kick you off the ranch?"

"Sure, but he always says the same when my decisions don't match his."

"You don't sound worried."

He kissed her again. "I'm not. He isn't going to control me the way his father controlled him."

"What about your mother? Will she support us being together?"

Brushing strands of light blonde hair from her face, Wyatt couldn't resist another kiss. "She's a huge fan of yours. I believe she's also tired of dealing with Pop's continued feelings for your mother."

Confusion tightened the lines around her mouth and eyes. Wyatt watched the changing emotions on her face.

"What is it?"

"Anson doesn't still love my mother. The fact is, he's been barely civil to her since I was old enough to notice. He might still feel guilt at how he hurt her, but your father's been in love with your mother forever. My mother reminds Anson of his failure to stand up to your grandfather. How easily he let go of the woman he'd planned to marry." Stroking fingers over his jaw, she could see the flash of pain on his face. "Your father loves Margie. I believe he has for a very long time."

Jaw tight, he swallowed the knot of truth in Daisy's words. His father wasn't a bad man. He'd been a good, if hard, father. In Wyatt's memory, he'd always been a devoted husband.

"We should join the others before Pop or Mom come looking for us." Helping her off his lap, he took another moment to hug and kiss her. Threading his fingers through hers, he opened the door, leaning down to whisper something in her ear. His reward was a genuine smile, making everything in his world right.

"How are you, Daisy?" Margie stood by her side at the largest of the dining tables. Name tags had been set at each place. She stood in front of Wyatt's spot. On one side was Dorie's name and on the other side was a woman's name Daisy didn't recognize.

"I'm good. Thanks so much for inviting Lily and me to join your family."

"You're always welcome here. I saw you come out of my study with Wyatt. I'm so pleased to see you two together."

Turning to face the crowd by the buffet table, Daisy spotted Wyatt talking with Virgil. "I hope our relationship doesn't cause problems."

"If you're talking about Anson, don't worry. You and Wyatt deserve the chance to decide if you have a future. I'll make sure he doesn't interfere."

Daisy appreciated Margie's support. She also knew no matter the woman's assurance, Anson could make Wyatt's life miserable.

"Come on. I'll introduce you to some friends from out of town. I've already told them about your shop, and they're anxious to see it."

Wyatt's heart clenched as he watched his mother and Daisy walking toward a group of people. He winced at what he'd told her. The days he'd taken to soul search their relationship had produced surprising results.

The magnitude of how much he missed her provided insight into the extent he cared about Daisy. While riding the fence line, he'd mentally listed what he liked and didn't like about their growing relationship. The list of things he didn't like ended up being so short he discarded it.

By last night, when he'd read her text messages, Wyatt knew he'd fallen in love. Whether or not his father approved, he found himself believing marriage would be in his future.

Virgil and Lily were talking again, this time at one end of the table laden with appetizers. Wyatt figured their brief conversation would end as had the other times he'd seen them together.

Their conversation would turn to the past, when Virgil ended their relationship to attend college. Wyatt had done the same with Daisy, the difference they'd been dating a few weeks, while Virgil and Lily had been together two years.

Out of the corner of his eye, Wyatt sensed someone approach. Stifling a groan when he saw it was his father, he steeled himself for the conversation to come.

"How are you doing tonight, Pop?"

"I'd be better if that Raines woman hadn't come. Who invited her?"

"I did. You need to get used to us being together, Pop."

"Why? Do you plan to marry her?" The sneer in his voice set Wyatt on edge.

"Maybe."

Crossing his arms, Anson turned toward him. "You can't be serious."

"I'm not ready to ask her, but you need to know she means a great deal to me. I'd appreciate it if you'd take some time to get to know Daisy. She's a good woman, Pop."

"I'm going to call everyone to dinner. Are you two ready?" Neither had noticed Margie joining them. "Wyatt, I've changed your seat so you're sitting with Daisy, Virgil, and Lily. You don't mind, do you?" She smiled as she asked.

"Not at all, Mom. Thanks. I'll go find them. Pop, please consider my request." Wyatt clasped his father on the shoulder, winking at his mother before going in search of Daisy.

Margie slipped her arm through her husband's. "You aren't giving him a hard time again, are you, Anson?"

"He's not thinking clearly about that Raines woman."

"Our son is thinking with his head and his heart. You've taught all our sons to stand by their convictions."

"This isn't about convictions. He's letting his heart rule him, not his head, Margie. The woman is wrong for him."

"The same as her mother was wrong for you?" She held onto his arm when he tried to pull away. "I know she loved you very much, but you made the decision to break off the engagement and marry me. There have been many times I wished you'd stuck with your convictions and married her. The reality is, you didn't."

Seeing the color on his face turn a deep red, she softened her voice. "Wyatt has chosen a different path than you. He wants to continue his relationship with Daisy. You have to accept his decision on this, Anson, or you run the risk of him leaving. We both need him here.

Besides, I've already put a deposit on a cruise starting two days after Christmas."

"Jonah and Gage will be home for the holidays. They can run the ranch if Wyatt leaves."

She squeezed her husband's arm. "Don't be ridiculous. Neither has a heart for the ranch. Not like their brother. If you don't believe me, ask them."

"They aren't here or I would."

"They'll be here as soon as the storm in eastern Wyoming passes. Don't be surprised if they make it in time to enjoy dinner." As she finished, the front door opened, their sons stomping off the snow before stepping inside.

Releasing Anson's arm, Margie heard a distinctive groan as she hurried to her youngest boys.

"Are you thinking of marrying Daisy?" Jonah sipped coffee, stuffed to overflowing from all the wonderful food. Gage sat next to him on the sofa in their mother's study, while Wyatt and Virgil were in chairs across from them.

"Don't get ahead of yourself, Jonah. I care about her, but marriage at this point is a stretch." Wyatt clutched his large mug with both hands, hoping they didn't hear the unease in his voice. They didn't need to know marrying Daisy had taken a prominent place in his thoughts.

"This isn't about me and Daisy. I want to talk about the coming changes at the ranch."

Jonah's brows drew together. "Is there more than what you've already told us? My understanding is Gage and I will need to help more at the ranch because of Pop's health."

"There is a little bit more."

Virgil choked, setting his mug down, working to hide his grin. "Excuse me."

Gage leaned forward, resting his arms on his thighs. "All right, lay it on us, Wyatt."

"I've met with the bank manager and the assistant manager about what I'm going to tell you. Virgil already knows and has added his input."

Over the next half hour, Wyatt explained his thoughts to add a dude ranch and western living options to what the ranch already offered. Jonah's expression remained unreadable, while Gage loved the idea of sharing the outdoor activities and ranch life experiences with city people.

"So, instead of Nacho and Emma cooking every meal, the guests could choose if they want to participate, even helping to plan meals. Do I have it right so far?" Jonah glanced at the others, who nodded.

"Would that be part of the western experience you want to provide, Wyatt?" Gage's legs bounced up and down, a sure sign what his oldest brother described excited him.

"I believe so. When we have a chance to list all the activities we're able to provide, we'll be able to categorize them for marketing purposes."

Jonah gave a slow nod. "And Pop has approved all this?"

"He doesn't know anything about the plans. Unless the bank manager has told him. If you two agree to be a part of the changes, I'd suggest we meet with him and Mom before you leave."

Gage moved his gaze to Virgil. "How do you fit into this?"

"I'll be doing much of what I do now."

"So you'll continue being in charge of the breeding, training, and sales programs?" Gage asked.

"That's my understanding. You already know Jasper has been diagnosed with asthma, which saps his energy. He can't work as many hours each day, but he'll still plan the work schedules for the ranch hands."

Jonah rubbed his hands together, weighing everything he'd heard. "You'll still be helping Virgil, right, Wyatt?"

"Definitely, but Virgil will be in charge of that part of the ranch. As I mentioned, Gage will be in charge of the western experience part, and you will handle all legal and financial matters. You've already finished your law degree, and you'll have your MBA by May."

Jonah's expression remained impassive. "Yes." Of the four, he appeared to be the least inclined to go along with what Wyatt proposed.

Gage shot Jonah a look. "You don't seem too interested."

"Not quite true. My concerns are the increased expenses and number of people we'll have to hire. Do you think Nacho will stay?"

Jonah's question was a good one. Nacho often grumbled about feeding the family and ranch hands. The change could mean adding up to fourteen guests each week during the late spring, summer, and early fall.

Wyatt gave a slight shake of his head. "I don't know. He's been hinting at moving to Arizona. What do you think, Virgil?"

"He's our wild card. There's no family other than an older brother who lives south of Tucson. It will take months to get our plans ready to launch, which will give him time to make a decision. His assistant, Emma, is very capable. She's worked in the restaurant industry since graduating from a culinary school. I can't recall which one. We'd have to allow her extra time for her son."

"What about her husband?"

Virgil looked at Jonah. "They're divorced."

The room quieted for several long moments before Wyatt broke the silence. "What do you think?"

Gage's smile brightened the pensive mood in the study. "The ideas are great. We'll need to complete the details and figure the money required, but I'm for the changes. Jonah?"

"I can put numbers together, and check on any legal issues we might face. Our biggest obstacle will be Pop. You know how much he hates change." Jonah sent a pointed look at Wyatt. "I'd say we talk to Mom first, get her approval, then we sit down with Pop." Standing, he held out his hand, a conspiratorial grin brightening his features.

A moment later, all four held their hands out as they did as boys, each one stacked on top of another. Their gazes locked on Wyatt.

"Ready? One, two, three."

The four cheered, sealing their decision.

Chapter Twenty-Five

"Thank you for coming today, Daisy." Wyatt slung an arm over her shoulders as they walked to her car. "It may be a few days before I can see you again."

Leaning into him, a deep wave of affection enveloped her. "You need time to visit with your brothers."

"We're going to speak with Mom tomorrow, then talk to Pop."

"About your plan to open a dude ranch?"

"Yep. Jonah and Gage support it. With Mom's support, there's a good chance Pop will give the plan a chance."

"If there's anything I can do, all you have to do is ask. I'm good at building websites, and marketing."

"Aren't you already busy with your shop? I don't want to take advantage of you." Wyatt would love to have Daisy involved.

"I'll have time after the first of the year. Will you need help before then?"

"No, other than letting me bounce ideas off you."

"You can do that anytime you want, Wyatt."

Stopping next to her SUV, he wrapped both arms around her. Bending down, he covered her mouth with his, hoping for more time before Lily joined them.

The sound of the front door opening ended their kiss earlier than he wanted. "Save next Friday night for me. I'll let you know if I can get away sooner."

"I'll save Saturday for you too." Her smile always shed light on any darkness plaguing him. Right now, Wyatt felt a huge amount of confidence their ideas would be realized.

"You and Virgil spent a good deal of time together." Daisy didn't want to push, but was dying to know what they talked about.

Lily kept her hands clenched tight in her lap, back straight, and her gaze not wavering from the road ahead. "They were short conversations. I asked about the ranch, his duties, if he ever planned to attend veterinary school."

"What did he say?"

"What did you expect? There's no money. If he had the funds, his preference would be to attend Colorado State University." Lily stared down at her hands. "I offered to help. He turned me down before walking away. That's the last time we talked today."

"Are you talking about the life insurance?"

Lily nodded. "I've never touched a dime of my parents' life insurance money. I mentioned loaning it to him. He could pay me back once he had a job after graduation. You would've thought I'd slapped him. We may not talk again for another eight years."

Daisy glanced over in time to see Lily swipe a tear from her face. "Give him time. Virgil's a proud man. He'll need time to think about your offer."

Gripping the steering wheel, she thought about the plan Wyatt, his brothers, and Virgil would present to Margie and Anson. If accepted, Virgil's experience and skills would be essential for success.

"I still love him, Daisy. It's been eight years, and nothing has changed. Us talking today only means we're finally able to be friends. As far as anything more, I don't see it happening."

"What are you saying?"

"This is so hard, but I think it's time for me to move on." Lily's voice broke on the last, remaining shaky as she continued. "I've turned down invitations by eligible men for years, hoping Virgil would realize he still loved me. It never happened. As much as it hurts, it's time to give up and create another dream."

"I'm so sorry. I thought, hoped, if you two could talk, you might be able to work it all out."

"It's been too long. Much too long."

Slowing her speed, Daisy leaned forward in an attempt to see around the coming curve. The road was slick with ice, and cloaked in total darkness without a hint of the moon.

As her fingers tightened on the steering wheel, a large truck rounded the corner ahead of them, moving into their lane. Headlights blinded Daisy for an instant, yet that was all it took for her to tap the brakes, sending the SUV into a skid.

Screams filled the vehicle as she worked to get her vehicle under control. Turning into the skid, she had little time to think before they hit the berm, lifting the SUV enough to send it down the steep embankment.

Slapping her thighs, Margie turned her gaze toward Anson. "Well, I think these are great ideas. Wyatt spent eight years working on Emmett and Lucinda's dude ranch, learning every aspect of the business. With Jonah's degrees in law and business, plus Gage's degrees in recreation and tourism, the boys have what's needed to make the new ventures successful."

Anson scowled at his wife, then the others. "And what of the breeding and training operations? We can't ignore what's been our bread and butter for decades."

"I was just coming to that, Pop." Wyatt pulled a paper from the stack of backup information the four had stayed up all night to create for this meeting. "Virgil will continue heading up those operations. I'll be helping him, plus focus more attention on sales."

"I want to be involved in both the dude ranch and western experiences."

All eyes locked on Margie. "Mom, will you have time with traveling and the rest of your work on the ranch?"

She waved his question away with a flick of her hand. "We won't be gone all the time, and I'll make it a point to be around during the busiest part of the visitor season. I'm concerned Nacho won't stay."

"We have bigger issues than our cook leaving." Shoving up from his desk chair, Anson paced by the window. "This is still my ranch, and whether we make changes or not will be my decision. Right now, I haven't been convinced we need any of what the boys are proposing."

Wyatt, Jonah, Gage, and Virgil exchanged glances. They hadn't expected him to dismiss their ideas without reviewing all the documents.

"Whistle Rock Ranch is *ours*, Anson. Have you forgotten we're fifty-fifty partners?"

Jaw going slack, he stared at his wife. "You'd go against me, Margie?"

"We need to keep evolving if the ranch is going to stay viable. What they're proposing is a great start, deserving serious consideration."

"I've heard nothing to make me want to get behind their plans." Anson's gaze moved over the group, seeing disappointment and disbelief on their faces.

Rising, Wyatt pointed to the stack of papers. "Those are copies. It would be a darn shame to miss an opportunity because of pride. Jonah and Gage are returning to campus on Sunday. You have almost two days to review the proposal and ask questions."

"And if I don't?"

Letting out a weary breath, he shook his head. "We all have options, Pop."

As the others rose, planning to leave, Wyatt's phone rang. Pulling it out, the I.D. showed Brilliance Hospital.

"This is Wyatt Bonner."

"Wyatt, this is Gabe Montez." Gabe was a few years older, a friend, and a doctor at the local hospital.

"Hey, Gabe. What can I do for you?"

"Do you know Daisy Raines?"

Gripping the phone, he walked several feet away from the others. "She's my girlfriend. Why?"

"There was an accident. She's in critical care, along with one of our nurses. Lillian Cardoza. Lily said Ms. Raines has no family in town. They were in an accident. She mentioned your name."

"We're on our way." Whirling around, he locked gazes with Virgil. "We're leaving. Daisy and Lily had an accident. They're in critical care."

Anson watched the room clear, choosing to stay away from the hospital. He'd spent too much time in intensive care this year.

Turning from the window, he spotted the stack of papers on the small conference table. His boys and Virgil had worked hard to prepare the information in less than twenty-four hours. He appreciated their hard work, the way Wyatt and Virgil had obtained Jonah's and Gage's commitment. Both were natural leaders.

Closing the distance to the table, he pulled out one of the heavy wood chairs and sat down. Pulling the stack toward him, Anson started at the top, reading every page, each footnote, and studying the graphs he assumed Jonah prepared.

An hour passed as he studied the information, writing down his questions on a notepad. Finishing the last page, he leaned back, rubbing both hands down his face. He wasn't certain how long he sat there, contemplating what to do.

Anson didn't take change well. No, that was an understatement. He hated change, couldn't see the need for it. If something worked fine for fifty years, he saw no reason it wouldn't work another fifty. He knew his views were old-fashioned, often keeping the ranch from improving.

Drumming fingers on the table, he stared down at the cover page. *Whistle Rock Dude Ranch and Western Adventures.*

Virgil had explained they wanted to tie the new operations to the original ranch while leaving no doubt about what was offered. Jonah suggested the dude ranch be part of a new corporation, separate from Whistle Rock Ranch.

Reviewing his list of questions, Anson read each one, making additional notes. He tried to see it from their point of view, hard for an older man so set in his ways.

The ranch had done well over the years, surpassing his and Margie's expectations to become one of the most successful operations in Wyoming. Both loved breeding and training horses. Whistle Rock Ranch had become a premier provider of Paint horses. Customers came from all over the world to purchase Bonner stock.

Anson understood the business, could talk to anyone about their horses. Now he faced expanding into areas he knew nothing about.

Margie had made it clear she supported their efforts. She'd always been one to try something new while dragging him along with her. He loved that about her. Her adventurous nature had them pursuing actions he would've walked away from.

Anson thought of the land required, new buildings, additional ranch hands and administrative staff. The boys recommended starting slow. Knowing them, the word would spread like wildfire.

Blowing out a breath, he grabbed the phone on the table. The person he called picked up on the second ring.

"It's Anson. We need to talk. Yes, today. I'll be there within the hour."

He had one more call to make before leaving. "Good, you're in. There are two patients in critical care. Daisy

Raines and Lily Cardoza. You let me know what their insurance doesn't cover. And make sure they have decent food. Not the overcooked slush from the cafeteria."

Ending the call, Anson sat for a moment before heading to his bedroom. He had a lot to do and not a great deal of time.

Chapter Twenty-Six

The five people from Whistle Rock Ranch came in separate vehicles, parking together in the hospital lot. Wyatt and Virgil took off at a run for the hospital entrance while Jonah and Gage waited for Margie.

"We're here to see Daisy Raines and Lillian Cardoza. Dr. Montez called me."

"Are you relatives?"

"Neither have family in the state. I'm Daisy's boyfriend and Virgil is Lily's."

Cocking a brow, the receptionist sent a disbelieving look at Virgil. "I've known Lily a while now, and she never mentioned a boyfriend."

Offering his most engaging smile, Virgil rested his hands on the counter. "We've known each other for over ten years. We recently got together." He figured it wasn't a lie since they had gotten together to talk several times at Thanksgiving.

"There you two are." Gabe Montez walked toward them, shaking their hands. Tall, lean, and strikingly handsome, he'd worked at Whistle Rock Ranch during high school, and summers while attending college. Anson had made it his mission to secure a place for him at the hospital after Gabe completed his medical training.

Wyatt wasted no time. "How are they?"

"Come over here. We'll talk before going to the back." He led them to a quiet corner, greeting Margie, Jonah, and Gage when they joined them.

"My understanding from what Lily told me is they were driving to town from the ranch when a truck rounded a corner and came straight at them. Their SUV skidded before going over the embankment. I'll tell each of you about their individual injuries when we get to the back. The main thing is, both will be fine, but will require care at home for a few days. Follow me. I know you're anxious to see them." Gabe gave Margie and Wyatt's brothers an apologetic look. "Only one visitor per patient for now."

Wyatt's heart thrummed inside his chest as he followed Gabe through the hallway. He didn't know how his father had handled being confined to a hospital room for weeks without losing his mind.

Gabe stopped, indicating for Virgil to wait while he took Wyatt to see Daisy. "She has a severe concussion, which is the most serious injury. Her left wrist is sprained, as is one knee. The airbags deployed, which saved both from more serious injuries. Because of the concussion, and sprained knee, she'll need someone to stay with her a few days."

"Would it be all right to bring her to the ranch?'

"That would be best. Margie and Nacho could help. Is there a chance Lily could stay there a few days?"

"Absolutely. This all assumes neither will fight us on coming home with me and Virgil." Wyatt stopped in his tracks when he saw Daisy.

Her head was wrapped in bandages, as was her wrist. Bruising colored much of her face, and her right eye was swollen shut. "Geez."

"It could've been much worse." Gabe pulled a chair next to the bed for Wyatt, who still hadn't moved. "I'll give you privacy while I take Virgil to see Lily."

Wyatt couldn't stop staring at the purple bruises and swelling on Daisy's beautiful face. Throat tight, he took measured steps to the chair, still unable to tear his gaze away. He should've followed her instead of being so anxious to explain his grand ideas to his brothers.

Reaching out, he covered her unbandaged hand with his. Closing his eyes, he sent up a prayer for her quick and full recovery, knowing God would hear him.

"You came." She croaked the words as if they were torn from her.

The rough voice had him picking up the cup with water and straw. "Of course I came. So did Virgil, Mom, Jonah, and Gage. Drink some water, sweetheart."

She did as he asked before sighing.

"More?"

"Not now." Her voice was still thready, although better than when she'd first spoken. "My head is pounding."

"You have a concussion. It'll take time to heal."

"I want to go home."

"Gabe hasn't released you to leave. It may be another day or two."

"Gabe?" She touched her temple. "Oh yes, I remember." Closing her eyes, she drifted off.

Watching Daisy breathe in and out, he had no desire to leave her side. Dragging the chair closer, he covered her free hand, once again chastising himself for not following her home. Maybe he could've done something to avoid the accident, or lessen the damage.

"Don't blame yourself, Wyatt. You couldn't have changed the outcome." Jonah set a hand on his brother's shoulder. "Did you talk to her?"

"For a minute. When Gabe releases her, she'll need someone to keep watch and help her get around."

"Bring her to the ranch?"

Wyatt grinned up at the most serious Bonner son. "I'm guessing she'll fight me, but I don't see a better solution."

"Why don't you take a break and go talk with Mom and Gage? You can mention bringing Daisy home. You know Mom won't have a problem with it. What about Lily?"

Standing, he continued to watch her, still accepting the damage to her body. "Her too. Virgil won't want anyone else staying with her."

Jonah grinned, glancing between Daisy and Wyatt. "It could be a fight with both of them."

Walking to the door, Wyatt cast a glance over his shoulder. "I'm looking forward to it."

"Do you have anyone else who is able to stay with you for several days?" Gabe shoved his glasses up his nose, meeting Daisy's hostile glare. When she didn't respond, he made a note in his tablet. "I didn't think so. I'm recommending you and Lily be gracious and accept the Bonners' offer to have you stay with them. They have plenty of room, a cook, and people who can check on you several times each day and at night."

"I don't like it."

"Didn't expect you to. Lily's already agreed to go."

Daisy tried to sit up, without success. "She did?"

"As a nurse, she understands the need to have someone close while recovering from a concussion. It shouldn't be more than a few days. Think of it as a holiday. You get to stay in the Bonner lodge while enjoying homecooked meals. Plus, you'll be fussed over by Margie, Wyatt, and Virgil."

"I don't like to be fussed over."

Finishing his examination, Gabe made notes in his tablet before giving her a meaningful look. "Don't fight this. Your other option is to stay in the hospital."

Groaning, her mouth twisted in a grimace. "Not much of a choice."

"Wyatt already put a sign on your door about being closed until one in the afternoon, when your help comes in. He also left a note for them to call him. You're lucky to have the Bonners as friends."

She knew he was right. Maybe this would be her chance to win over Anson.

"When can I leave?"

"Wyatt and Virgil will be here anytime. They took Margie by your house and Lily's apartment to get clothes. I'm afraid yours were ruined in the accident."

They looked behind Gabe at a knock on the door. A young man with a handful of flowers stood by the door, looking as if he wanted to be anywhere but in the hospital.

"Is this Miss Daisy Raines's room?"

"It is. And you are?"

"Jimmy French. I, um...well..." Realizing he hadn't removed his hat, he swept it off his head. "I'm the driver of the truck."

Gabe turned to face Daisy. "This is Miss Raines."

Taking a few steps into the room, Jimmy held out a handful of winterberry stalks. "I'm real sorry, ma'am. My truck slid on the ice. I sure didn't mean for anything to happen to you."

"Good intentions don't go far when the deed is already done." Wyatt's voice came from behind Jimmy, causing the young man to whip around.

"I know, sir. I'm terribly sorry. Mama said I should bring flowers, so I picked these on the way to town. There aren't any real flowers right now, and I didn't have any money, so I hope these are all right." Face turning red, he looked at the berry stalks. His face twisted into an embarrassed frown. "You could maybe make jam?"

Daisy worked to stop the laughter bubbling inside. She couldn't recall the last time she'd heard such a sincere apology, even if they did bring a scowl to Wyatt's face.

"That's very nice of you, Jimmy."

As a smile formed, he closed the distance to her bed, setting the stalks on the end of her bed. "I, uh...don't have insurance. You probably already know that. But if you owe money, I can work it off. The thing is, I don't have a job right now."

Biting her lower lip, Daisy shot a look at Gabe, then Wyatt. "Well, I'm not sure—"

"You'll be following us to the Bonner ranch, Jimmy. The work is hard, and two hours per day of your wages will go to Miss Daisy and Miss Lily. You good with that?"

Brows rising, he looked as if he'd won the biggest prize at the state fair. "The Bonner ranch? Heck, yes, I'm fine with it. Mama won't believe me, so you might have to call her."

For the first time since arriving at her room, the corners of Wyatt's mouth twitched. "Have you been to Miss Lily's room?"

"Yes, sir. She was real nice, but the man with her didn't take to me too well."

"Virgil will get used to you."

"Virgil?" Jimmy reached into a pocket, pulling out a well-worn piece of paper. "Virgil Redstar?"

"Yes. Why?"

"The man at the feed store told me to talk to him about a job working with the horses. I was driving out there after Thanksgiving with Mama."

"Wasn't it a little late to come visiting?" Wyatt's features relaxed the more the kid talked.

"I was gonna sleep in the truck so I'd be there at sunrise. Guess that idea didn't turn out too well."

"Well, I'd better get on to my other patients. Daisy, you call me if you start feeling dizzy, have stomach cramps, or the headache gets worse. Wyatt has a list of instructions, and I've ordered medications to take with you. I want to see you a week from today. My office, here at the hospital, at ten in the morning. Don't make me come find you."

"Yes, sir," popped out before she had time to think. "One week from today. Got it."

"Wyatt. Get in touch if there are any changes."

"Will do. And thanks, Gabe."

The nurse appeared, pushing a wheelchair. "Ready to get out of here, Daisy?"

"No offense, but absolutely."

Chapter Twenty-Seven

"Doc Montez has cleared Lily and Daisy to go home tomorrow." Virgil stood next to Wyatt outside the circle pen, watching Jimmy exercise one of the Paints.

Though it hadn't been long since hiring him, Jimmy had proved to be a good addition. Wyatt hoped he wouldn't disappoint them as time passed.

The abnormally warm weather right after Thanksgiving had melted much of the snow, leaving several areas on the ranch compound available for training. It had taken the men an hour to spread hay throughout the round pen, transforming the thick mud to a manageable surface for working with the horses.

"I know what Gabe said."

"What are you going to do?"

Blowing out an exasperated breath, Wyatt tightened his grip on the top rail of the pen. "About what?"

Stepping from the bottom rail to the ground, Virgil leaned against the fence. "It's not my business."

"No, it isn't." Wyatt shook his head at the clipped response. "I don't know what I'm going to do. The last few days have been perfect. Even Pop has made an attempt to talk with her." Removing his hat, he fingered the brim while gazing out on the spectacular landscape. Settling it back on his head, he accepted the truth. "I'm not ready for her to leave."

Virgil said nothing at first. He knew how Wyatt felt. His relationship with Lily had improved during her brief stay. They needed more time to decide if they could be more than friends. "Daisy doesn't have to go. At least not for long."

Wyatt wasn't so certain. His affection for Daisy had grown to the point he no longer wondered about being in love. He did love Daisy. She brought light and laughter to his sometimes challenging existence.

She loved horses and the ranch. Wyatt's mother and brothers would welcome her into the family. The question remained whether she loved him enough to build a life together. He knew one way to find out.

"You good here?"

Virgil's expression signaled the answer.

"Right. Dumb question." Jogging toward the house, he vaguely heard Virgil's shouted, "Good luck." Waving his hand in the air, he headed to the kitchen door.

Stomping his boots, he stepped inside, stomping them again on the rug. "Morning, Emma. Is Nacho about?"

"Hello, Wyatt. Nacho planned a trip for supplies and volunteered to take Koa to school. He should be back soon. Can I help you with anything?"

"Not right now. Is my mother still at her meeting?"

"As far as I know. Your father went to town with her. Something about business he had to finish."

Lifting a brow, Wyatt glanced away, perplexed at Emma's response. "I'm heading upstairs to speak with Daisy. The doctor has cleared her and Lily to go home. Virgil plans to go with me. We'll wait until my parents return. Do you have time to make lunch for the ladies before we leave?"

"If chicken salad or turkey sandwiches are all right, I've got you covered." Emma smiled as she said it. Over the days since she'd arrived at the ranch, her personality had begun to emerge. Wyatt believed she'd be a great addition to their staff.

"Great. I'll let you know the timing."

Taking the stairs two at a time, he walked down the hall. Passing the first bedroom where Lily had been staying, he stopped in front of the last door. Grimacing, he reversed directions toward his bedroom.

His eyes scanned the room, stopping on a velvet pouch next to a picture of him and Virgil on his dresser. Heart thumping, he loosened the string, removing his grandmother's engagement ring. Designed out of yellow gold, a beautiful diamond had been surrounded by small sapphires. If the story his father told him was accurate, his grandfather won it in a poker game years after marrying his grandmother. He hoped Daisy would like it.

Slipping it into a pocket, he forced out a deep breath while returning to her room. The sound of two voices came through the door. Lily and Daisy were together. Not quite the ideal scenario for asking a woman to marry him.

Knocking, he heard steps approaching before the door swung open. Lily stood inside, one hand on her hip.

"Hey, Wyatt. Come on in." Pulling the door wide, she looked at Daisy. "I'm going to pack so I'm ready for the drive home. Virgil mentioned leaving after lunch. Is that right?"

Wyatt stared at Daisy, her blonde hair piled on top of her head in a messy bun, her hands fidgeting with the edge of the blanket. She'd never looked more beautiful.

"Wyatt?"

"What? Oh, yeah. After lunch."

Lifting a brow, she shot a look at her best friend before leaving.

"Morning, Daisy. How are you feeling?" Grabbing one of several wood chairs with tapestry seat covers, he set it by the bed.

"Great. I still need to take a quick shower, then I'll be ready to go home." Continuing to play with the blanket, she let her gaze roam over Wyatt.

The last few days had been bittersweet. He'd hovered in her room the first two, before Margie shooed him out to get his work done. She knew from talking to the doctor her injuries were a little more serious than Lily's. The knowledge had relieved Daisy's conscience. It wasn't her friend's fault she'd failed to keep the SUV on the road.

The words about going home were true. Still, sadness harbored in her chest, knowing she wouldn't see Wyatt as often. She'd grown accustomed to his bedside visits, their talks while he held her hand, and his kisses before leaving her to rest.

Daisy found it easy to envision a future with him, their children running along the halls, learning to cook from her and ranch chores from Wyatt. She'd fallen asleep thinking of them being together. Today, though, was about partings, and the thought caused her heart to squeeze.

"Virgil mentioned the two of you driving us back to town."

"Right."

"Emma is a real nice lady. So is her son, Koa."

"Yeah, they are...nice."

Cocking her head, Daisy studied him. Rarely did she have to pull words from him. Today must be special, she mused to herself, feeling little joy in the task.

"I saw you and Virgil working with Jimmy. How's he doing?"

"Jimmy? Uh...fine."

"Do you think he'll stick around at the ranch?"

Shrugging, he continued to stare at the way her hands played with the blanket.

"Wyatt?"

"Yeah?"

"Are you all right? You seem to be miles away."

Taking a moment to answer, he searched for the courage which surrounded him as he walked down the hall to her room. It must've fled, the same as his voice.

"Should I have Lily get Margie?"

When the words penetrated, his body jerked, shoulders squaring. "Heck, no. Besides, she's in town with Pop. I'm fine...real fine."

Reaching out, he took one of her hands in his. His thumb rubbed circles on the back.

"Something isn't right. I'm going to get Virgil." Her attempt to throw off the covers failed when his hand gripped her wrist.

"No. I'm fine. Really. Just, uh...give me a minute."

"One minute. Then I'm having Lily get Virgil."

One minute. Sixty seconds. Wyatt figured he could deal with that. Drawing in a slow breath, he held it a few seconds before letting it out. Once more, and he felt pretty good, his courage returning. He couldn't put it off any longer or she'd shout for Lily.

"You know how much I care about you, right, Daisy?"

Brows drawing together, she gave a slow nod. "I guess so."

"Do you care about me?"

"You know I do."

"Good, because I more than care about you. I love you." He hesitated at her quick intake of breath. Squeezing her hand, he leaned closer. "Your image is on my mind when I fall asleep and wake up. I think about you all the time. The fact is, I can't stop thinking about you."

Seeing a tear form and fall, he stopped, unsure what it meant. Lifting his hand, he swept a strand of hair from her face.

"I love you so much, Daisy, I can't see a future without you." Reaching into his pocket, shaky fingers retrieved his grandmother's ring. "Mom gave me this the first night we brought you here from the hospital. It belonged to her mother."

Locking eyes with her, he took her left hand. "Marry me, Daisy. Be my best friend, lover, and the mother of my children."

Tears streamed down her face, a sob breaking loose.

"Do you love me, Daisy?"

She nodded, a smile tilting the corners of her mouth up as another sob escaped.

"Do you want to marry me?"

Nodding again, she took the ring from his hand, slipping it on her ring finger. Another sob broke loose on her answer. "Yes!"

Chapter Twenty-Eight

Holding her on his lap, Wyatt kissed Daisy as if she'd disappear if he let go. Her sobs subsided, replaced by low laughter. First from her, then Wyatt.

Ending the kiss, he rested his forehead against hers, a broad smile focused on her. Neither spoke for a long minute, as each realized the commitment they would be making.

"You surprised me." Daisy swiped at the moisture on her face.

Chuckling, he stared into her bright, green eyes. "I surprised myself."

"Yeah?"

"For an instant, I didn't think the words would come."

"Why not?"

"Fear you'd say no."

Her features relaxed, eyes softening at his admission. "And here I thought nothing scared Wyatt Bonner."

"You'd be wrong, sweetheart. You're at the top of the list."

"I'm not scary."

Chuckling, he kissed the tip of her nose. "You have no idea."

Wyatt meant it. Nothing frightened him more than Daisy Raines. Not even the upcoming announcement to his family about their engagement.

Daisy placed kisses along his jaw, wiggling to get closer to him.

"Daisy?"

"Hmmm..."

"That's not a good idea." Lifting her, he set her on the edge of the bed. "We have to talk about what comes next."

"You're talking about Anson, right?"

"Yeah. I don't know how he'll take the news."

"Badly. He doesn't want us together. I'm afraid our marriage could throw him into another heart attack." She placed her hands in her lap, worry obvious in the way they shook.

Placing a calming hand over hers, he tried to reassure her. "Mom will be behind our decision. So will everyone except Pop."

"Maybe he'll surprise us."

"Don't count on it." Walking to the window, he saw his parents park their large SUV and climb out. "They're back from town. We need to be prepared for any reaction."

"All right. You consider his reactions while I take a shower. I'll meet you downstairs. Besides, I need time to admire my new ring." Holding up her left hand, she wiggled her ring finger as she twirled in a circle. "It's so beautiful."

Stalking to her, he grabbed her around the waist, continuing to twirl her. "You're the one who's beautiful."

Setting her down, he kissed her once more. "Don't forget I love you."

She ignored the slice of worry flitting through her. "Or that I love you."

Daisy rushed through her shower, dressing in pants and one of the sweaters Margie had brought from her house. Combing her long hair into a ponytail, she admired the ring one more time before going next door to Lily's room. Knocking, she walked in.

"You're packed."

"It's time I got back to my job at the hospital."

"You don't look too anxious to leave."

Sitting on the edge of the bed, Lily stared at the stunning Aubusson rug on the polished wood floor. "My life is in town." Forcing a smile, she shifted toward Daisy. "What is that on your hand?"

Rushing toward her, she grabbed Daisy's hand, holding it up. "Tell me."

"Wyatt asked me to marry him!"

"Oh, my gosh. That is so wonderful." Tugging Daisy into a hug, she tightened her hold before letting go. "The ring is absolutely gorgeous."

"It was his grandmother's." Holding up her hand, she again admired the stunning design.

"Have you discussed a date?"

"Not yet. We want to make the announcement, and know what we're up against. I wish Anson didn't hate me so much."

"Oh, Daisy. I don't believe he hates you. He's scared about how he'll react if you're a permanent part of their lives. I love Margie, but it's Anson's own fault for giving up your mother without a fight. He needs to man up and put the past behind him."

"Guess we'll find out what he plans. I'm pretty certain Wyatt intends to share our engagement today." Walking to the door, she pulled it open. "Let's go downstairs and get lunch. I'm starving."

Partway down the stairs, voices from the kitchen drifted upward, Anson's being the loudest. "Sounds like a full house." Daisy's stomach clenched tighter the closer she got to Wyatt's father. Crossing into the kitchen, she let Lily go first.

"You're okay. Wyatt and Anson are talking on the other side of the room." Entering, Lily led her to the far end of the large center island.

Spread out were ham, turkey, and chicken salad sandwiches on various breads, a large bowl of sliced fruit, tortilla chips, salsa, and fresh guacamole. At the other end was a plate of still warm brownies, plus oatmeal, lemon, and snickerdoodle cookies.

Taking a plate, Daisy selected half a sandwich, adding tortilla chips and a small scoop of guacamole. Behind her, Lily did the same. Both moved to the side of the room,

Daisy watching Wyatt while Lily's gaze landed on Virgil, who stood close to Emma.

Appetite disappearing, she tossed her plate in a nearby container, more than ready to leave. For the last few days, Virgil had been the one to sit with her, wake her during the night, making certain she ate, and drank copious amounts of water. All of his attention stopped this morning after the doctor pronounced her and Daisy ready to go home. He'd abandoned her as if she'd become an anchor around his neck.

"You tossed your food away. Are you feeling all right?"

"I'm great. Just anxious to get home. Will you be staying or going with me?" Lily shot a quick look at Virgil, who still spoke with Emma.

Lily couldn't blame him. She was a beautiful woman, with an oval face, large brown eyes, and golden brown hair cut to just below her jawline.

It had been silly for her to believe she and Virgil were growing closer over the last few days, maybe putting the past behind them to start again.

"I'll find out soon. Wyatt wants me to join him and his father. Wish me luck."

"Always." Lily moved into the background, ready to grab her belongings from upstairs and leave as soon as Wyatt and Daisy made their announcement.

Across the room, Virgil's gaze kept moving between Lily and Emma. He'd seen her dump her food and move into the shadows, as if she'd bolt any second. It didn't make sense. They'd talked for hours over the last few days in an attempt to ease the pain from their past.

He planned to drive her home after lunch, and get her agreement to go out to dinner with him. Virgil had no intention of letting the progress they'd made go to waste. Seeing her scoot even farther into the shadows, his intention to join her stopped at the sound of Anson's booming voice.

"Seeing as how we have a full house in the kitchen, Wyatt would like to take a moment to make an announcement. Son?"

Taking Daisy's hand in his, she inched closer to him, still stunned by Anson's seeming acceptance of their engagement. She couldn't help wondering if and when his true feelings would show.

"This may seem short, but it has been a long time coming. Some of you know Daisy and I dated in high school. Coming back to the ranch, I was determined to see her again. We've spent a good deal of time together the last few weeks. So, to cut this short, I'm very pleased to announce Daisy has agreed to be my wife." Holding up her left hand, she showed off the family engagement ring to applause and shouts of congratulations. "There's no date set, so don't ask." Leaning down, he brushed a kiss across her lips. "We'll have a party to announce our engagement, but we wanted family and close friends to know first."

Margie hugged both of them, followed by Anson. Virgil came up next, sweeping Daisy into his arms and slapping Wyatt on the back. When finished, he searched for Lily, disappointed to not see her.

Not worrying about it, he turned his attention back to his friends, a smile breaking out across his face. He had plenty of time to talk Lily into seeing him again. Today was about Wyatt and Daisy, two people he loved very much.

Epilogue

Four months later...

Wyatt stood in the reception line, holding Daisy's hand as they greeted family and friends. He would've preferred a quick wedding on the ranch, followed by a long honeymoon in one of the luxury lodges in Yellowstone. Seeing her now, stunning in her off the shoulder white wedding dress, he conceded all worked out for the best.

The church had been filled to standing room only, the same at the large reception room on the lake south of Brilliance. The early spring day had turned out perfect, with wildflowers dotting the area around the event center.

"Congratulations. The two of you are perfect together." Dorie hugged Wyatt, then Daisy. "I'm so happy for you." Moving on, the town veterinarian had a broad smile, yet her shoulders slumped enough for Daisy to notice.

"I hope she finds someone, Wyatt. She truly is a lovely woman."

Squeezing her hand, he agreed. "She will, sweetheart. Looks like she was the last in line. Let's get out of here."

Tugging on his hand, she laughed at his rush to get her alone. "Not yet. We have to mingle, take more pictures, dance, and have cake."

"We should've eloped," he mumbled as she led him to a group of Whistle Rock ranch hands.

Lily watched them from her table not far from the band. Soon, they'd start the dancing with a two-step.

The last few months had been difficult for Lily. Between the store, seeing Wyatt, and planning their wedding, Daisy had little time leftover for other socializing. As the maid of honor, they'd shopped for dresses, but instead of being asked to help with flowers, the cake, invitations, or anything else, Margie had taken over.

To fill the time, Lily took on more shifts at the hospital, and took cooking classes she'd normally attend with Daisy. Virgil had been absent since she'd left the ranch after the accident.

She'd seen him at the Bonners' on Christmas, but he'd spent most of his time talking with Emma. He did take a moment to thank Lily for a book she'd given him on holistic doctoring for animals, apologizing for not getting her a present. Yet he had given Emma something, as well as a present for her son, Koa. It had been a painful lesson in letting go. She hadn't returned to the ranch since.

Her New Year's resolution had been to date anyone who asked. She'd lost count of the cups of coffee, lunches, and dinners she'd shared with single men. There were two she continued to see when their schedules allowed.

"Would you care to dance with me, Lily?"

Her chest heaved at Virgil's strong, deep voice. Pulled from her thoughts, she saw his hand reaching toward hers.

"I, uh…"

"One dance."

"Just one?" Her traitorous heart overrode her mind as she realized one wouldn't be enough.

"Yes."

"All right."

After being on the dance floor less than a minute, Lily realized her mistake. Virgil hadn't asked out of desire to be with her. He'd asked because she was the maid of honor and him the best man. The obligatory dance between the two. The instant the song ended, she thanked him before walking back to the table.

Before sitting down, Virgil's hand gripped hers. "We need to talk."

"I doubt Emma will want to be away from you much longer." Wrenching her hand free, she left Virgil standing on the edge of the dance floor.

"Do you know where Lily went?"

Confused, he looked at Daisy, shaking his head. "She walked through the door in the corner. We aren't getting along right now."

"Of course you aren't. Not after all your attention has gone to Emma the last few months."

"What are you talking about?"

Crossing her arms, Daisy studied his face, wondering how he hadn't figured it out on his own. "Are you still interested in Lily?"

Staring at the ceiling to calm his frustration, he looked back down at her. "You know I am."

"Well, I have to say that surprises me. Instead of you driving her back to town after our accident, you opted to stay at the ranch and spend time with Emma. At Christmas, you gave presents to Koa and Emma, and forgot Lily. I know for a fact, you haven't made the effort to see her since. She and I thought after all the attention you paid her while we recuperated at the ranch, you were trying to get back together. Seems we were wrong. I'd better go find her, Virgil. If you still have an interest in Lily, you better find a way to get back in her good graces before one of the single men she's dating sweeps her away."

Speechless, Virgil watched her leave. Single men? Dating? He'd been so busy doing his work at the ranch and working on making the dude ranch a reality, he ignored his interest in Lily.

"You look as if you've been punched in the gut." Wyatt clasped his friend on the back.

"Feels as if I have. Daisy set me straight on how I've treated Lily."

"She's been itching to say something for weeks. Sorry. I thought she'd wait until after we got back from our honeymoon."

"Don't be sorry, and don't hang around here with me. Find your bride and enjoy the rest of the party." Virgil drew him into a bro hug, then stepped back. "It's your day. Make the most of it."

"I intend to."

Virgil scrubbed a hand over his face as he watched his best friend go in search of his bride. He'd felt horrible about forgetting a gift for Lily while making sure he had presents for Emma and Koa. His only excuse was they hadn't exchanged presents since before he left for college.

Did Lily really believe he had feelings for Emma? Thinking back to November and December, he winced, closing his eyes. His actions had pushed Lily away, creating a mess he had to fix.

No matter what it took, he'd get Lily back. And this time, he'd never let her go.

Learn about upcoming books in the Cowboys of Whistle Rock Ranch series at:
https://www.amazon.com/gp/product/Bo9RCQK4TF

Enjoy the Whistle Rock cowboys? Here's another series you might want to read the Macklins of Whiskey Bend.

If you want to keep current on all my preorders, new releases, and other happenings, sign up for my newsletter at: https://www.shirleendavies.com/contact-me.html

A Note from Shirleen

Thank you for taking the time to read **The Cowboy's Road Home**!

If you enjoyed it, please consider telling your friends or posting a short review. Word of mouth is an author's best friend and much appreciated.

I care about quality, so if you find something in error, please contact me via email at shirleen@shirleendavies.com

Books by Shirleen Davies

Contemporary Western Romance Series

MacLarens of Fire Mountain

Second Summer, Book One
Hard Landing, Book Two
One More Day, Book Three
All Your Nights, Book Four
Always Love You, Book Five
Hearts Don't Lie, Book Six
No Getting Over You, Book Seven
'Til the Sun Comes Up, Book Eight
Foolish Heart, Book Nine

Macklins of Whiskey Bend

Thorn, Book One
Del, Book Two
Boone, Book Three
Kell, Book Four
Zane, Book Five, Coming Next in the Series!

Cowboys of Whistle Rock Ranch

The Cowboy's Road Home, Book One

The Cowboy's False Start, Book Two, Coming Next in the Series!

Historical Western Romance Series
Redemption Mountain

Redemption's Edge, Book One
Wildfire Creek, Book Two
Sunrise Ridge, Book Three
Dixie Moon, Book Four
Survivor Pass, Book Five
Promise Trail, Book Six
Deep River, Book Seven
Courage Canyon, Book Eight
Forsaken Falls, Book Nine
Solitude Gorge, Book Ten
Rogue Rapids, Book Eleven
Angel Peak, Book Twelve
Restless Wind, Book Thirteen
Storm Summit, Book Fourteen
Mystery Mesa, Book Fifteen
Thunder Valley, Book Sixteen
A Very Splendor Christmas, Holiday Novella, Book Seventeen
Paradise Point, Book Eighteen,
Silent Sunset, Book Nineteen
Rocky Basin, Book Twenty

Captive Dawn, Book Twenty-One, Coming Next in the Series!

MacLarens of Fire Mountain

Tougher than the Rest, Book One
Faster than the Rest, Book Two
Harder than the Rest, Book Three
Stronger than the Rest, Book Four
Deadlier than the Rest, Book Five
Wilder than the Rest, Book Six

MacLarens of Boundary Mountain

Colin's Quest, Book One,
Brodie's Gamble, Book Two
Quinn's Honor, Book Three
Sam's Legacy, Book Four
Heather's Choice, Book Five
Nate's Destiny, Book Six
Blaine's Wager, Book Seven
Fletcher's Pride, Book Eight
Bay's Desire, Book Nine
Cam's Hope, Book Ten

Romantic Suspense

Eternal Brethren, Military Romantic Suspense

Steadfast, Book One

Shattered, Book Two
Haunted, Book Three
Untamed, Book Four
Devoted, Book Five
Faithful, Book Six
Exposed, Book Seven
Undaunted, Book Eight
Resolute, Book Nine
Unspoken, Book Ten
Defiant, Book Eleven
Consumed, Book Twelve, Coming Next in the Series!

Peregrine Bay, Romantic Suspense

Reclaiming Love, Book One
Our Kind of Love, Book Two
Edge of Love, Book Three, Coming Next in the Series!

Find all of my books at:
https://www.shirleendavies.com/books.html

About Shirleen

Shirleen Davies writes romance—historical, contemporary, and romantic suspense. She grew up in Southern California, attended Oregon State University, and has degrees from San Diego State University and the University of Maryland. Her real passion is writing emotionally charged stories of flawed people who find redemption through love and acceptance. She now lives with her husband in a beautiful town in northern Arizona.

I love to hear from my readers!

Send me an email: shirleen@shirleendavies.com
Visit my Website: https://www.shirleendavies.com/
Sign up to be notified of New Releases:
https://www.shirleendavies.com/contact/
Follow me on Amazon:
http://www.amazon.com/author/shirleendavies
Follow me on BookBub:
https://www.bookbub.com/authors/shirleen-davies

Other ways to connect with me:

Facebook Author Page:
http://www.facebook.com/shirleendaviesauthor
Pinterest: http://pinterest.com/shirleendavies
Instagram:
https://www.instagram.com/shirleendavies_author/
TikTok: shirleendavies_author
Twitter: www.twitter.com/shirleendavies

www.ingramcontent.com/pod-product-compliance
Lightning Source LLC
Chambersburg PA
CBHW071229210726
48293CB00002B/634